LILIES OF THE DAMNED
WRITTEN BY OSCAR VIVARIUM

Elsewhere Publishing

Any resemblance to real persons is purely coincidental. All characters appearing in this work are fictitious. Any resemblance to real persons, dead or alive, past or present, is purely coincidental.

Text copyright © Oscar Vivarium. All rights reserved. No part of this book may be reproduced of transmitted in any form or by any means, electronic or mechanical, including photocopying, recording, or by any information storage and retrieval system without written permission from the author.

Cover designed by Elsewhere Publishing

First printing
01/08/2024

Dedicated to the source of my unending love

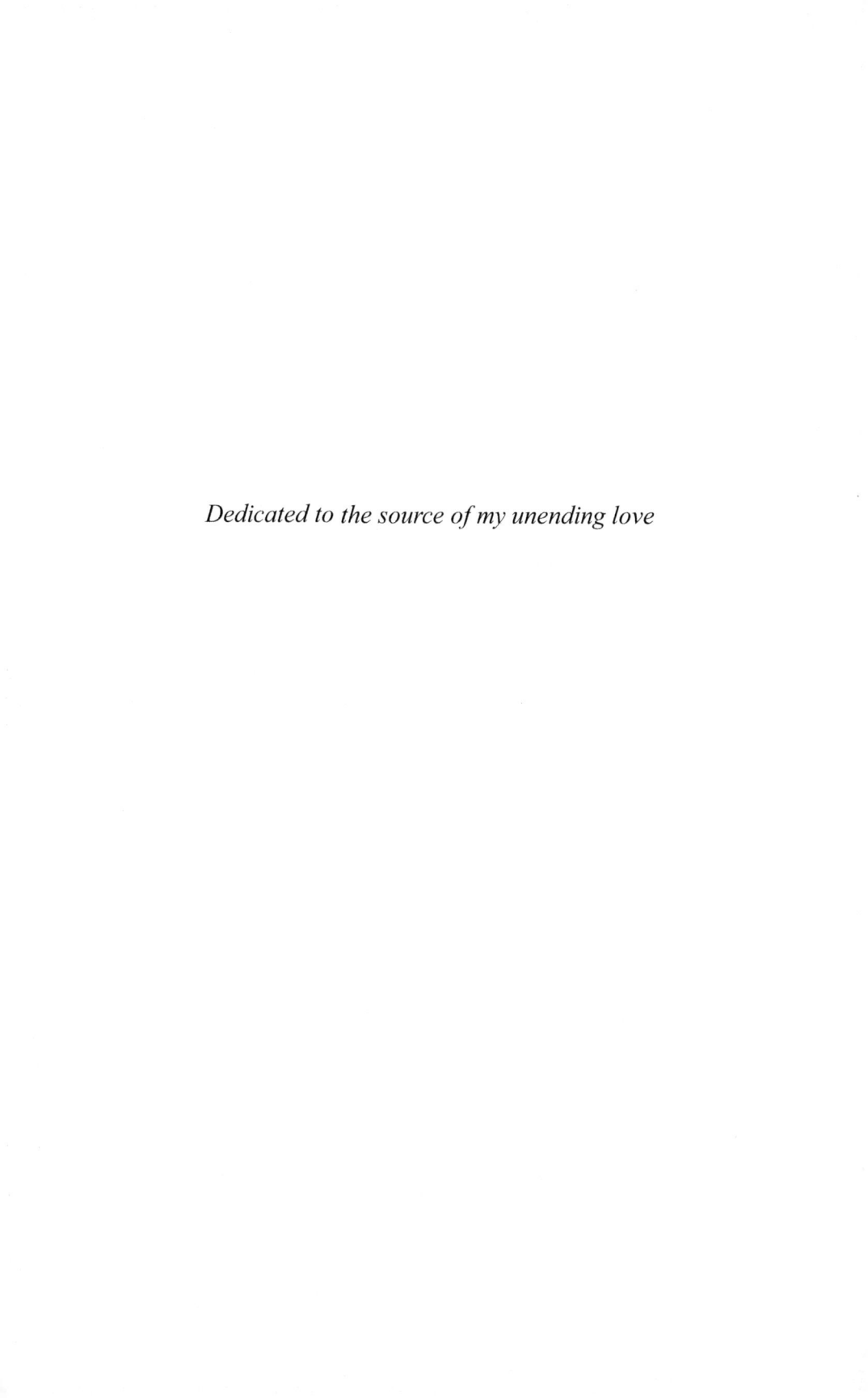

LILIES OF THE DAMNED

PART ONE - INFATUATION

CHAPTER ONE

CONCEPTION

Who would dissuade the blossom of love one feels in their breast for another ensnared spirit? Any who walk this plane with their beholder, who may touch, feel, see, and adore, should be so fortunate. To cherish a reflection of their lover in their mind's eye, and to hold it dearer than truth. It is a blessing that one should indulge in the solipsism of love, and some may even find themselves with these feelings in isolation, with none willing to share them. For love is the loneliest of all things, and the most important thing is to be desired, known only by those who are not.

Oscar sat upon a metal railing, musing. He rocked gently, swinging his legs back and forth beneath him. He believed his mind lucid enough to see forming patterns and draw parallels with all things. In truth, he did not know whether this was a symptom of the creative force, or dormant madness. These two ideas did not have to exist in contention, though.

A bus came to a halt before him, and he became acutely aware of the surrounding eyes. He suspended his thoughts and dropped down from the railing as the burgeoning crowd formed a queue. He let any bystander who looked vaguely interested in the line take precedence and gripped his ticket assuredly, rehearsing what he might say to the bus driver out of the corner of his mouth; when comfortable with his words and tone, he bowed his head.

His interaction with the driver pleased him, and a flash of sweat only permeated his brow when he walked past those seated to the stairs, to which he darted up, bundling himself into a corner at the back of the bus.

He placed his backpack next to him as though it were a shield, and hoped profusely, it needn't be moved. Yet, as the bus slowed to a second stop, milling bodies made their way upstairs; their extremities clambering for seats, causing Oscar to eye his surroundings apprehensively. To his satisfaction, many ahead of him begrudgingly moved their possessions aside.

He allowed his head to fall to the window beside him, nursing his temple against the glass. He delved once more into the reaches of his mind's eye, scrutinising his thoughts for reprieve. He pondered the topic of his fixation, refusing to understand how one could be so open in their being with another. And to do so in a way that permitted intimacy! He scrambled for a point of relatability drawing from his own existence, and tried to be as honest as one might be with themselves; a scowl appearing across his face, his nose scrunching and his eyes disappearing between his cheeks and brow.

An elderly man two rows ahead of him turned to open a window above. Oscar tapped his fingers aggressively against his knee, unsure if the man had seen his drawn expression, and if he had, would he take offense?

He sighed, awash with the summer breeze. The bus rocked comfortingly across the potholes of the country roads ahead, cradling his thoughts.

He awoke before his stop.

He was always intrigued by how one was able to rescue themselves from a nap so opportunely.

He thanked the driver and departed from the bus, shooting up the hill to his home. He unlocked the front door, ran upstairs and punched his bedroom wall, unconvincingly.

He did not want to break his hand but did want to chastise himself enough for riding the bus home at nineteen. Some days this concerned him more, depending on if he was trying to court at the time. He would weigh up how much his ineptitude would affect the make-believe relationship, and how the subject of his desire would view him if this truth were to be revealed.

Careful not to touch any of his possessions, he walked to the bathroom, knocking his mother's cardigan from the top of the wash basket. He dumped his backpack on the floor next to his jumper and scrubbed at his face fervently with his fingernails over the basin, slapping back any escaping water onto his face.

He dropped his pants to his ankles and kicked them over to his jumper, before hopping under the shower. He blasted frigid water over himself to see how long he could withstand it, having read online that cold showers were supposedly good for you; he did not doubt this but had yet to see or receive any tangible results from doing such. That said, he only managed to remain under the water for around twenty seconds each time; for he feared he may enter a state of hypothermia if he were to remain any longer.

He turned the heat up almost immediately and placed the plug in the basin hole. He slid down the tub so that he lay flat on his back and let the water cascade over him. He looked up to the ceiling and masturbated, lying in a mire of his own filth until suitably miserable.

Once washed, he withdrew a fresh set of clothes from the bottom of his drawer and dressed himself, looking out across the suburban vista from his bedroom window.

'Fuck off'.

The reprimand was not directed at anyone, more, at himself, if a candidate had to be put forward. He cursed once more through gritted teeth, suspecting a neighbour might hear him if he were to be any louder. This release did not ease his being, instead, it brought tears to his eyes. He looked out to the livid red sky; the sun was setting like an amber jewel, and he watched it descend until it vanished from the horizon so that he was alone under the dark heavens.

How many more of these days could he endure? He did not wish to die but had respect for those who managed such a feat. He would scour forums late at night, always with great concern someone was viewing his browsing from afar and that they would tell his loved ones of his ignoble searches. Or, that this information would somehow find its way back to his family; perhaps by anonymous email, or something inconspicuous, like a letter demanding their attention resting at the foot of their door. He would search via an incognito tab, all the while still convinced this form of browsing did nothing to veil his searches from the web overlords.

He would read forum posts until he found one that brought him to a splendour of tears. Usually, a post from one who had lost a family member, or a child to suicide. Oscar found solace in the words of strangers, but not to the point it would forever stop his quandaries. As when the following day came, he would once again become a slave to his inhibitions.

He recalled the first funeral he attended; for his friend's father. And upon this reflection, thought it strange that he attended the funeral of one he had never met. It was as though a celestial force was delicately showing his young mind the emotion of grief, so that one day he might cope better. As though it whispered to him in his ear: 'Here! Imagine how awful this would be if it was someone you knew? Thankfully it is not—for now!'

The funeral was for the father of his friend, Fred, who had hung himself in his flat. But one week prior, he had ridden the bus to meet his son in town, turning up obscenely drunk. This was the last physical interaction his son had with him, and upon his father's return home, he messaged Fred, telling him he was loved.

Oscar recalled being present when Fred's mother told her son the news. They were staying at a friend's house together, drinking and smoking into the early hours of the morning.

'He's gone.' Were the only words Fred spoke to him, his bottom lip trembling, and his heavy frame becoming unbearable to him; his large face bearing down into his cupped palms.

The funeral struck Oscar as a strange affair from the moment he arrived. The atmosphere of which was not sombre, and instead held an undercurrent of excitement that refused to dissipate. The stubborn aura remained throughout the course of the ceremony, leaving him to wonder if he, too was guilty of such exhilaration. Most of those in attendance were his school peers, their boyish faces riddled with awe and their hair cropped over their small skulls by a mother's touch.

Yet, Oscar thought if he were able to act in an appropriate manner at that age, then why were his friends not able to? It was as if the ceremony took on the same proclivity as a field trip.

It was a dire affair in all, as when presenting the lifeless body of Fred's father to the audience, the pallbearers dropped the coffin, leading to a resounding clunk as the casket smashed against the ground. Those who did not know previously, were now made acutely aware; Fred's father was a giant man.

Upon reminiscing, Oscar acclimated to his situation. Life was not all bad; he knew at the least, rock bottom was not yet a prevailing sentiment. Refreshed by a nostalgic sensation of grief, he declared to himself he did not wish to feel like this anymore. He refused to waste his formative years spiraling, and tonight, instead of his usual resignation, he would sleep with a newfound lust for existence. Although he knew come morning, he must again return to his dish, and eat it cold.

Oscar jumped between the sheets of his bed and yearned for the time betwixt twelve and one o' clock to play out eternally, so that he may have all the time he required. He stayed awake until the early hours, reflecting on a particular instance that had transpired on his last day of college earlier: his English teacher, Miss Hallowes, had leant over his shoulder and pointed to a passage in his book: On The Road by Jack Kerouac. The exact line eluded him, something about a 'spider in the night sky', but it left a pleasant impression, nonetheless.

His teacher's arm remained outstretched as she dropped her collarbone aside his neck, allowing her coiled raven locks to fall upon him, enamoring him. Her face was perfectly rounded and cute, resembling the shape of a heart; her features shy and her voice warm. Her intimate arrival had made Oscar apprehensive; he did not want to disgust her, and turned to see her breasts hanging forth, curtailed by her black silk top. He could not tell if she was wearing an undergarment and did not risk a confirming look, turning his gaze downward to his book. He felt asynchronous with those around him, as though suspended in a neat pocket of time with Miss Hallowes. He remained still, concerned by his breath, holding it tightly in his chest. She pushed herself against him and he could smell her jasmine scent. To him, it smelt perfect, as did the scent of any perfume.

He yearned to take her in that moment, and wondered if she was aware of this. Would his teacher do such a thing on purpose? She was awfully close. He was unsure of how long their interaction lasted, or what was said amidst the exchange, all he knew was that he desired her intensely.

He gratified himself again, wiping his seed on a tower of surrounding pillows. He remained still for a moment, and then rushed to the bathroom to wash his hands.

He thought to send her an email, alluding to his affection, cloaked in the guise of kindness and appreciation for her help throughout the year. It was not that he did not value her—quite the contrary. He cherished her spirit; her wit was exemplary, and her charm intoxicating. But his sexual perversion for her was too great to refrain from such desires in writing, and all efforts to do so would surely damage her idea of him.

He turned his phone to face his darkened window, probing the back of the device with his finger, before scrolling through his contacts, all the while waiting for his phone to die. And to his lack of surprise, his charger was not working. He squashed the charger wire under his phone between his mattress and bedframe, in the hope it would suffice.

The light of dawn was now creeping through his window; the insidious chirping of birds had begun. Alas, it was done. The college year was over, and Oscar would have to decide which sea he would sail on from hereon.

As he drifted between the waking world and a dream, a final memory surfaced. He recalled the social media post of a dying young man, or boy. The indistinguishable truth of his age added to this person's mythology in his mind. It was a viral post from some years ago; the post concerned the boy's dying wish, to raise money for a charity. But despite his frustration, he could not remember the person's name, yet vividly remembered the image attached to the post: the boy wore glasses and a hospital gown and held his thumb up to the camera with a careful smile upon his weathered countenance. A smile that might inspire one to climb over a trench and run headfirst to certain death, but not to make a charitable donation.

It sickened Oscar, that those who once fawned over the dying boy would no longer do so. He thought this might be unfair, as surely this death would have left an irreversible impression on the boy's family. But he located his disdain immediately. His seething was of course not aimed at the family of the victim, it was directed at those who leeched the victim's life force to the very end. Those who made a show of feigned comradery to the dying boy, reposting and providing their useless postulations of guilt. He hated these people most of all. By way of example, he hated these people more than serial killers. At least serial killers had individuation; he decided he did not hate serial killers.

Oscar hoped by thinking of the boy, it would allow an apparition of his form to permeate this waking realm, in some fashion. He was not sure how this would work, or if it did, but he was gladdened by the sentiment he posed. In truth, he thought of the boy more than his deceased grandfather. He was ashamed by this but struggled to amount the grief required to equate the two all the same.

This was his last dreamlike pensive.

Oscar awoke to a ringing sound from an already ruined sleep. He had experienced the type of rest, where one is unsure if they ever slept. He reached between his bed frame and plucked his phone from its burrow.

Fred was calling him; usually he would not pick up, but there were times when he did. This time, he justified his reasoning as such: there was no requirement for him to be anywhere today and he could go back to sleep immediately after the call.

'What's up?'

After a delay, Fred replied distortedly, 'you Good?'

'Are you off your nut?' asked Oscar.

Another delay. The pause gave him apt reason to believe this was the case.

Fred snorted an embarrassed chuckle. 'What are you doing?'

Oscar scowled under his covers. He was more frustrated with himself than Fred. What did he expect, after all?

'I thought you might have been in trouble, why else would you ring at this time? There are two reasons that you might: you're off your nut, most likely. Or something important. Which, to be honest, is so fucking stupid of me to even assume. Because if you were in a twist, you wouldn't be ringing me, would you?'

'People think I was born yesterday don't they,' said Fred, in a tone only reminiscent of a grumbling drunk.

Oscar exhaled.

'Are we going out tomorrow, yeah?'

'It is tomorrow, you fat fuck,' said Oscar.

'Tonight then?'

'I may as well.'

Fred pursued him: 'The old Admiral, is it?'

Oscar conceded.

'Are you wanting to stay at mine after? My Mum isn't back until tomorrow night. Shit, she might even be back next week, I can't remember,' said Oscar.

'Can do sheriff.'

'Can do sheriff or yes sheriff?'

'Yes sheriff. Is your weird mate coming?' Fred asked dryly.

'He's not my mate, he's your mate,' Oscar grinned, hiding behind the glare of his phone that shielded him from the encroaching light of day.

'He'll be going if you're going, won't he? He loves you mate.'

The joke played out for some minutes between them, at the expense of their friend.

'Fucking Richard you know,' Oscar said, before continuing. 'Enough of this shit dude, you need to go to bed, or you'll flake later—won't you?'

'You know me, I'll always be about. I've just downed a bottle of wine; my mum is fucking fuming.'

Oscar forced a show of laughter down the speaker.

'Right, shall we call this a day?'

'Don't you worry about her,' replied Fred in a stupor.

'Do I sound worried about her?'

'Oi, I'll finish this bottle, the—'. Oscar hung up and dashed his phone across the room. He cursed under his breath, then got up to retrieve it. Whilst stood, he hastily texted Richard, letting him know that Fred had called. He hoped his message might wake Richard up, so he might also share in his dismay. He followed up with another text, mentioning that they were meeting up later in the evening for a 'big sesh', before returning to bed.

PART ONE - INFATUATION

CHAPTER TWO

THE SEED

Hot rays permeated Oscar's window and beams of light pooled into his room, confronting him with a choice. He could either lower his blinds and attempt to go back to sleep, or he could admit defeat and start the day. It was one o' clock in the afternoon, and the march of Summer was upon him.

Depressing, Oscar thought, as he acknowledged the time on his phone. He tried to shove the head of his charger back into it at another angle, hoping it would last the day.

He treated days like this as dispensable. It was the first day of a summer holiday that would not be ended by a return to education, but by winter; the first day of the rest of his existence.

He ran his hand through his hair, his fingers becoming enmeshed within his coarse locks. His chin rested upon his chest that rose and fell gently as he considered the day ahead. He became fixated on the festivities which marked the evening, mulling over the potential events of the night; formulating a reaction to all hypothetical situations which may or may not take place. Or, in another timeline had already happened an infinite number of times, each featuring their own microcosmic nuances, adjusted and repurposed for each simulation.

Oscar relented with the notion of purpose. He would fret over a list of theorems; questioning if he was part of the cellular makeup of a cosmic giant, or the avatar of an ineffable being, or something in between. To delve into such topics for any length of time would overwhelm him, causing a groaning feeling in his chest. He was envious of others, their distinct lack of care for truth, or at least the optics of it. These ruminations would last for days, until a new set of ideas were presented by his mind, to be again, soon displaced. At this time, he became cold and distant, but knew this to be his own doing. Despite his cognisance, he still did not believe he had the agency to act differently. At times, he would experience bouts of pronoia; one occasion saw a white pigeon fly to his windowsill on a dreamy afternoon, it was here that Oscar was convinced the bird had come to inform him that he was the chosen one.

After coming down from this state of mania, he was able to see this unlikely. Yet, he would be lying if he was to deny the small part of him that believed.

Today, no visions of grandeur perturbed him. He looked through his wardrobe, plucking out the garments he would wear later. The Admiral was a hive for locals and underage drinkers, there being only one police officer who lazed through the town of Kellwell at any given time. Letting much of the petty crime, if any were to occur, take place undisturbed. If you were to be kind to the officer, the job could be seen as an adequate substitute for retirement, providing a reason to postpone one's death.

The town of Kellwell itself, was a leafy suburb, and the only trouble that occurred, was usually related to debauchery. The school children amusingly referred to the lone officer as 'steady Eddy'. Eddy would never give chase, and instead opted to walk everywhere. To the point of such persistence that on winter's eve, he was pelted with snowballs by a crowd of underage drinkers on his evening stroll. Each time he approached the children, they ran back to regroup, sending another snowy volley his way. Like a man with an unquenchable desire for justice who had nowhere to be, Eddy pressed on.

Oscar was unsure how many arrests Eddy had made; he was yet to see one. He hoped one day to attain the inner peace that Eddy had, instead of waging psychic warfare upon himself.

He muttered under his breath as he pulled the last piece of his outfit from the closet. He would never be this age again, but strangely, this always filled him with glee. He recognised there would be a day in which he would outgrow late night escapades, but this would not be today nor any day soon. He looked to those who were older than him; some by ten, twenty, thirty, even forty years, who still frequented drinking establishments. Reaffirming his belief that he certainly had a good chunk of time to play with.

He headed downstairs, deciding to shower later. For now, he wore a tee, shorts and a cap, and made his way to the kitchen

'Carpe Diem,' he said to himself facetiously, as he grabbed a bottle of beer from the fridge.

After three beers he loosened up and took opportunity to message a selection of girls he went to college with, in hope of striking up a lukewarm tipsy exchange.

He glanced out the living room window, leering at the larimar sky above, squinting his eyes at the fierce blue. He was in two minds; to remain inside in the cool, or head outside to frolic. He chose to pace around the house lonesomely, kicking bundles of socks as he passed them by. But, as he patrolled the halls of his home, the beauty of the outside shone through to him pleasantly, softening his heart. He headed out to the front of the house, shuffling about the driveway in his socks, ducking under dapples of shade created by surrounding trees.

He swanned about the driveway, and clinked his bottle against a retaining wall, causing his beer to froth incessantly. He wrapped his mouth round the glass and the liquid contents shot up, hitting the back of his throat; making him cough, splutter, and finally wheeze for air.

Throughout this commotion, he hadn't noticed that a girl had passed him by. He only saw her now, walking ten feet ahead of him up the road. He was unsure if she had seen him or not. He thought she must have, but to save him from embarrassment, she might have pretended to not. Although he couldn't surmise if an action like this was part of her nature. With little choice, he played coy, retreating under a tree at the front of his home. Although the road was clear, it was an embarrassing affair for any passing ghosts to witness.

Though he could only see the back of the girl, she looked familiar. Her denim shorts caressed her curvaceous legs that bowed slightly inwards, and her thick pale calves gave way to her voluptuous careful frame. Her platinum hair both kinked and bobbed as she pushed against the curvature of the steep hill ahead; her skin rippling gently as she walked, her deft hands swinging gayly at her side, to and fro, framing her delicately groomed nude-coloured nails.

Oscar was wildly infatuated and spied on her for her beauty alone. For the first time in his life, he felt whatever represented his heart plummet to the bottom of his stomach. It was the same feeling one might have if they were informed of a lottery win, or that they had lost a loved one; truly, he believed that this feeling was more intense than the outcome of either fabrication. In another time, a war would have been fought for her hand.

From her fine form, he managed to place her. It was Eva Spring; a girl who attended the same college as him no more than yesterday. He had not looked at her in this way before, nor had she ever been revealed to him in such fashion. At college, she no doubt appeared to be a pretty girl by all estimations, but there, she wore outfits that covered her entirely. Not to say that these outfits were unflattering, but, prudent. Under the light of the sun, almost every inch of her beatific frame had now been granted to Oscar, and she turned momentarily to run a pale fae hand through her honey hair, revealing a diaphanous side profile of white gold and a nose ridge that looked to be delicately sculpted, like a button, complementing her full, rounded cheeks. Her eyes were like jades cut asunder from the bed of the sea and her lips were full and damp, glistening with a single bead of sweat. The light of day betrayed her momentarily, revealing her auburn roots beneath her crown. But to Oscar, this only added to the belle, and he had now visualised many futures in which they were together, as though in a half-dream.

She carefully stopped some way up the road to talk to an elderly man who awaited her. The man had a handful of grey hairs remaining atop his head and he tilted his chin close to his shoulder.

Eva looked shy as she stood still, but in a way that did not warrant concern, but more, suspicion of her surroundings. Oscar likened her temperament to that of a cat. He struggled to tell if she was aware of her beauty; he was not certain if all women were so sure of their charm.

He listened to her speak intently, her tone was excitable, and her accent thick and feminal. He had never heard her speak before, even at college, for the fleeting encounters that he had with her were only in passing, or an exchange that did not demand speech. He wondered if she knew him, if she had thought of him in any way that transcended formality on any of these sparing occasions. He thought to venture up the road, but decided he would appear as a freak.

Instead, he pretended to make himself look useful to no other than himself, pushing back some of the white flowers that bowed over his mother's wall. Quitting immediately, recalling his adverse reaction to pollen.

The old man handed Eva something; a steel object, Oscar guessed it a tray, but could not see the exchange play out in full. The old man said something, causing a flutter of excitement within her. Her laugh was like butter. She threw her head back and placed a hand onto her arched hip, revealing a portion of her buttock that protruded from the side of her denim shorts.

'Fuck,' Oscar whispered under his breath. He wrenched his cap downwards as to cover the front of his pasty skull and leant against the drive wall with one hand, imitating the action of a standing press up, before chugging down the remainder of his beer.

He became wholly dissatisfied; four beers provided a miserable experience. On this day, it was worth pushing through his dismay. He left the scene to retrieve another from the fridge. Normally, he would have let this lustful feeling lie, allowing it swell and then sink to the abyss of his subconscious, but he desired Eva unapologetically.

Oscar plunged his head into the basin of his sink, ejecting water from the tap onto his scalp. Removing his head only when every strand of his hair was drenched. He looked at himself in the mirror, fixated upon his hair that curled around his ears. To compensate for his unwanted mane, he had devised a concoction of two different hair sprays that he mixed with water. If done correctly, and applied almost immediately when his hair was wet, he was able to cake his head in the substance and stretch his hair into position, creating something that loosely resembled straight hair. The procedure must be done with ample time to spare; four hours was preferable, but two to three was also achievable depending on the humidity. The caked hair must be allowed to dry, becoming a crisp matt atop the head. He would use a towel to rub his crown until his locks simultaneously sprung forth from the clay hold. For a reason unbeknownst to him, this allowed him to style his hair in a peculiar fashion. Any alternative method to this, in his words, was 'absolute shit.'

He would not entertain shaving his hair off; going bald was the equivalent of suicide. Each time his mother suggested that he shave his head, it would be a topic of much contention. He tried to keep his method a secret for the most part, telling all who asked him about his straightened hair that he had a magic shampoo that relaxed his curls.

For the next hour he rubbed his head incessantly, until dust floated from his head forming a whimsical cloud around him. The worst thing that could happen at this point, was the realisation that not enough substance had been applied. However, in this case, he was pleased, and his hair was almost ready to be shown to the public. He ran his hand through his curls; his fingers now rummaging freely through his locks.

He coughed forcefully, attempting to eject any hanging dust from his lungs. He thought the byproduct of his Frankenstein might one day give him cancer.

His phone rang, and he clawed it from his pocket with his long nails, reminding him they needed to be cut; the upkeep to be presentable, was tedious.

He pulled his phone close to his face, squinting through the billowing dust.

'Y'ello.'

'Y'ello,' replied Richard.

'Hello! you're on the air.'

'First time caller, long time listener.'

'What's going on?' asked Oscar.

'I'm just driving.'

'Into a tree I hope,' quickly recalling that Richard's girlfriend was omnipresent. He preferred not to secure any risk of ill will at their pillow talk. 'Is Fran alright?' he added.

'No, she hasn't replied to me in days, if you know of her whereabouts, please let me know,' said Richard

Oscar took the speaker far away from his mouth, so that it would only just pick up his words and turned his head to the door to shout.

'It's nobody Fran.'

Richard laughed excitedly.

'What's the crack then,' said Oscar. 'I had that idiot ring me this morning, at like six. You didn't reply to my text.'

'Yeah, I know, sorry. I saw it and fell back to sleep.'

'I bet you did.' Oscar replied sardonically.

'Do you want me to come over to yours before we go to the Admiral?'

Oscar paused before speaking: 'I think my Gran and Grandad might be nipping to mine in the next couple of hours. I'll let you know when I can.'

'Okay, tell me when they're gone.'

'Will do,' Oscar said sheepishly.

He felt a tinge of guilt having lied, but he must have his hair appropriately placed before heading out. He went back to the fridge and pulled out two remaining cold beers. The comfortable flush of drunkenness was now enveloping his being. He returned to the front room and sank to the sofa, placing his hands onto his head; playing with a solidifying strand of hair that fell over his eye, thumbing it obsessively, moving it up and down between his palms.

He wondered if Eva would be out later and was wracked with both nerves and unadulterated glee at this prospect. He had no idea she lived close by, or even in Kellwell for that matter. He toyed with the idea of relieving himself but did not want to lose any potential testosterone he thought he had banked. His neck rested comfortably on the back of the sofa, as a myriad of blurred sequences played out before him. And so, he set sail upon these surreal shores for some time.

He was woken by his leg; it was tapping interminably on the floor. If his mother was present, she would have told him to stop this at once. But she was not, and this did not matter.

He ran upstairs, looking through the bathroom window, back up the street to where Eva's interaction had taken place. He looked at the spot where she once stood, half expecting to see her silhouette. She was not there, of course she was not. He wished for her to come back up the road, walking her perfect strut, so that he might have another chance to impress her. With a last leering look, he turned away from the window and entered his bedroom, prising the outfit he had meticulously placed earlier from his bed. What divine machinations were at play? he mused. If she was to be at the Admiral later; surely this would be a fateful encounter, one that was handpicked from a silver web of fate. Yet, it was a hot Friday and most of town's residents would be out in full force, and if his suspicion was correct, and she was to be a resident, then, it was safe to assume that she might be there. Though, he preferred the notion that it might be of fate's doing.

He dressed himself, and it was high time he contacted Richard; the lie had survived long enough. It was fast approaching five p.m, his hair was passable, and he had consumed his remaining beers. He rocked gently on the balls of his feet. He was acutely aware that Richard would know he had been lying; these white lies were sure to build resentment at some point, if not already.

Richard was driving when he picked up the phone. The pair exchanged a quip about how he was just driving around Oscar's house the whole time.

Richard confirmed he would be at Oscar's in fifteen minutes, but he was always late. His lateness was never enough to become an annoyance, more so an inconvenience. The kind of lateness where something only seemed amiss but was not abundantly clear upon arrival.

Richard arrived twenty-five minutes later.

Oscar opened the door and stood eye to eye with his friend. Richard's straw like hair appeared bleached by the sun; it resembled spiked reeds but had the texture of silk.

'Hola,' Oscar jested.

'Hola Señor. Where's Fred?'

Oscar's phone rang, but it died before he could answer it.

'Speak of the devil, that must have been him. Can you ring him? My phone is crap.'

'I can. But it's not your phone, is it? It's the fact you haven't charged your crappy phone.'

'Believe me, I have done! But my charger is wank.'

'I'll just order you a new one dead quick. It'll be here tomorrow, just ping me the money then?'

Oscar had fifty quid to play with, conveniently left by his mother.

'Nah, it's fine. Ring him though.'

'I'll ring him, then we're ordering you a charger.'

'Please don't order me a charger,' Oscar said with an expression of defiance that was now set upon him as stone. He turned and headed back inside, leaving the door open for Richard to enter as he pleased.

He pressed his palm into the tip of his nose gently and thought of Eva; his drunkenness serving only to proliferate the intensity of his rose-tinted memory.

Richard joined Oscar in the living room, but Oscar stopped him before he could take a seat.

'Make sure you choose your bed. Go chuck your bag on it now.' He said, pointing at the ceiling, as though Richard might levitate and pass through it.

Richard hopped up the stairs, and he heard his friend rummaging about his room, hearing the dull thud of Richard's bag hitting the spare mattress in the corner of the room. The mattress was positioned under a set of bookshelves nailed to the wall above. Richard always slept with his head directly under these shelves; he must have trusted in the sturdiness of the shelves, completely, or he was just young. Oscar's mother pleaded with her son, that if any guests were to stay, they would do so with their head placed at the other side of the mattress, lying the opposite way round. Oscar understood why Richard liked sleeping in this position, as he would do the same; the times that Oscar's sheets became too itchy to bear, he would also sleep on the mattress the opposite way round. Why would you want your head falling off the end of the bed, after all?

Richard returned, taking up a seat on the sofa to Oscar's left. Oscar preferred to sit on the sofa facing away from the large windows.

'Shall we get some booze? A couple crates or something,' asked Richard.

'We could fuck off Fred, and nip over now quickly? Actually, let's give it five minutes. What did he say to you on the phone?'

'I think his Mum is dropping him off, she won't be long,' confirmed Richard.

Oscar sprang into action: 'She's got a gammy leg, so she'll take ages.'

Rapturous laughter filled the room.

'The sheriffs, ya know,' Fred said upon entering the living room. He chugged from a bottle rosé; each word muted between gulps.

'Right, me and Richard are going to the shop. We haven't got anything to slurp on.'

He nodded to the bottle Fred held, and Fred waved it through the air as if directed by a conductor.

'I'll just wait in the gaff,' the drunkard said.

'You won't just wait in the gaff; we don't need you rolling about in here causing a scene.' Oscar looked to Richard, who was now entrenched as far as one could go within the sofa.

'Wait in the garden Fred, then I can lock the front door.'

'Are we leaving Freddo here then?' Richard inquired, pulling himself from his place of rest.

'Freddo ya' know,' mouthed Fred as he squinted, looking out the window to the brightness of day.

'Give me a second, nobody moves!' Oscar exclaimed and ran upstairs, ripping his phone from its charger; it was still dead. He jammed it back in and returned to his friends. Fred was now sprawled out on the wooden floor of the living room, trying to plug his phone into the socket behind the door.

'Fred, just stay in here, please,' Oscar said, eyeing his rhombus friend suspectly, 'Are we going in your car Rich? Or shall I give you a piggyback over?'

Richard gestured to Oscar's back, and Oscar crouched down to receive him playfully. They left Fred in the living room, hoping nothing would go awry in the fifteen minutes they planned to be out.

Oscar hopped into the front of Richard's car, and when the engine switched on, he immediately set about winding the windows down all the way. He waited until Richard reversed out from the drive and was on the road, before deciding to address him.

He bit his tongue, debating in his mind whether he would exaggerate his tale or not. No, he would not—he was trying to stop doing this.

'Can I use your phone dead quick?'

Richard pointed to it.

'There's this girl that goes to my college. Well, went to my college.'

'Oh yeah?' Richard replied.

'Yeah. I think she went to our secondary school; she might have been in the year below—I'm not sure.'

Oscar typed Eva's full name into Richard's search bar and thanked God it did not show up in his friend's previous searches. He clicked on her profile, looking as though a chunk of diamond had just fallen out of the glove box onto his lap.

'Look—what do you reckon?' asked Oscar.

Richard eyed his phone curiously, careful to not devote his attention entirely from the road ahead.

'Have you been speaking to her?' Richard gauged.

'Not really,' Oscar laughed. 'No. She's peng though.'

Out of respect, Richard did not agree entirely, nor did he dwell on it, chuckling awkwardly.

'She's alright, yeah,' Richard said, looking concertedly at the road ahead. 'Shall we just get a couple crates, or do you want some vodka as well? Have you got any mixer back at yours?'

The reply satisfied him; he did not want a great show of interest from his friend but did want to know if he should pursue this girl, as the inducement of his life's quest.

He sat still, attempting to quell his elation. He became increasingly frustrated with himself, lamenting his outburst of emotion. He always became most excitable about things that were just passing instances. It was in these moments, he was truly happy, the times in which the potential of tomorrow had not hurtled into the trepidation of the day.

'I don't have any mixer,' said Oscar.

Richard swung the car round a tight bend competently.

'Is that her?' Richard asked hysterically.

Oscar thought his friend was joking, but it was not in his nature to play coy with matters of the heart. He bolted in his seat, sitting upright, dropping his friend's phone to the floor, the phone disappearing between the front seat and the door.

'Fuck, sorry,' Oscar muttered to himself, whilst scanning the pavement Richard pointed to.

Indeed, it was her.

Eva walked towards them; in the same outfit she wore earlier. She was captivating.

Oscar ran his fingers through his hair and leant up against the open window, attempting to position his elbow on it, gingerly, so that he could reveal part of his face to her. He smiled, careful not to reveal his teeth, sucking his cheeks in marginally. He wondered if he might shout something, maybe call to her? He did not know. He settled with remaining silent, the option he would have chosen a thousand times over. He nodded his head to her as they approached, in a plight to appear reserved and uninterested.

Richard slowed down as they passed by, swearing to Oscar that it was not intentional, all the while, giggling childishly.

Eva looked up at the car; first to the driver, and then to Oscar. She proffered a timid smile across her doll-like profile, bowing her head before him, allowing her flaxen bangs to fall over her face.

They turned another bend, stopping in the corner shop car park.

'There you go!' Richard exclaimed as he pulled up the handbrake triumphantly.

'Yeah,' exhaled Oscar.

'She might be out later?' said Richard.

'You reckon,' Oscar replied. He tapped his nails against the glove box ferociously.

Richard left the topic alone. He knew Oscar well enough to surmise that the conversation was over.

On return, the friends dumped their loot onto the sofa. Fred was still lying in the exact same position he was in prior to their departure. The only difference being the bottle he once held, was now empty and rolled across the glossy wooden floor.

Oscar stood over Fred, looking down at him smugly, swinging his foot back and forth, as if to gesture he was kicking his ribcage.

'I know you're doing gear, but can you please, please, please, make sure to not leave a trace of it anywhere. That means no bags left out, okay?'

'Have you got the barn door key?' Fred asked, looking up at Oscar with wide eyes.

'Yes, I've got the barn door key,' Oscar plucked the relic of much infamy from his wallet and held it over Fred. 'I assume you want this barn door key?'

Fred pretended to be squashed by the sheer gravitas of the key, making a gargling sound and rolling about the floor. After finishing his display, he snatched it from Oscar's hand and buried it into a snowy bag he held between his index finger and his thumb. Fred looked at the bag introspectively, with only one eye open, sharing a startling resemblance with Al from Toy Story; the one who worked at the toy barn in the chicken suit.

Oscar had done coke before; not a great deal of times, but enough times. Enough to know that he didn't like it. However, this wasn't strictly true; he liked the idea of it, or at least from the outset, but after two hours on the stuff, he wanted to kill himself.

He recalled the time when his brother found him downstairs early on a Sunday morning wearing nothing but giant shades, sniffing lines from the dining room table. At this time, he was trying to write a novel and wanted to get as many words written as he could.

But when he lay asleep that night, he awoke, opening his eyes to reveal nothing but darkness. He thought then, he might have traded his sight forever for this experience, and so, after that day, he decided to stop. He had no issue weaning himself off things. And, in truth, he did not consider himself addicted in the least. Thought he believed it had its merits; he wasn't entirely sure what these boons were, yet.

He decided he might have some later, if Fred had not hoovered it all up by then.

'Did you get me anything?' asked Fred.

'We did,' chimed Richard.

'Pay him now,' Oscar said, looking at Fred intently.

'Yeah, I will.'

'Pay him now. Because I know you won't later, and you know you won't later,' said Oscar firmly.

The boys drank uninterrupted for three hours. In this time, Oscar was cautious to not let himself resort to a drunken spiel. The type that consisted of superficial words of love for those present, and the lengths to which one would go for their audience. Rounded off usually, with how one could not live without those in attendance; he hated doing such and proceeded to proverbially pummel himself the following day, while wrestling with his alcohol induced dread.

He was thankful there was only talk of degeneracy and slights taken at one another's lives in this time.

A motion was put forward to leave the house and head over to The Admiral by Fred. The group willingly left Oscar's abode, and mauve seams now permeated the skyline, blending with the azure of the day. The trio marched through the cool air of Kellwell, to which Oscar let out a triumphant sneeze, and his eyes welled up and turned a dark pink. His only response to such, was to pop a piece of chewing gum in his mouth.

The commotion outside the pub could be heard all the way down the street. The sound reinvigorated the lumbersome Fred; the noise giving him credence to rush ahead of his friends. He jogged forth and called back to them, asking them if they would be so kind to fetch him a drink. Then he picked up pace and disappeared into the horizon; his quest, to grab a pack of cigarettes or two.

Richard shook his head nonchalantly, dropping another button from his white shirt, before doing it back up again. Oscar felt impervious to his surroundings, and grabbed Richard by the scruff of his collar, pulling him through the swathes of people who milled outside the establishment.

As they made their way through the crowd, a burly figure with a receding hairline and a wiry black beard barged against them with a seismic force. The encounter took Oscar off guard, giving him barely enough time to pivot his weight to his back foot; only stabilising himself on the sea of surrounding bodies. He grabbed Richard's shoulder convincingly, making sure his friend was not subject to embarrassment.

The bearded figure continued past them, heaving his weight from side to side, toppling some of the daintier men who preceded him, and a handful of women beneath him.

'What the fuck was that.' Richard mumbled hazily towards Oscar's left ear, but Oscar was too perturbed to reply, whipping his head to the right to bear further witness. The bearded man had now forced his way into a makeshift ring of people. He had one of those bulbous necks, where there was an indented space for one's thumb at the back of it between the shoulder blades.

Oscar saw a figure pushed into the circle before the bearded man by the splayed hands of the masses, which then withdrew, having offered their yield.

The bearded man pulled the offering closer, who did not resist him. He gripped the left shoulder of the offering, steadying him, before sweeping a clenched fist across his jaw.

Oscar was unsure if the poor soul's jaw had been detached entirely; it now descended several inches away from his top lip, and from his gaping maw, gushed hot blood. The blood sprayed across the white tank top of the aggressor; seemingly affected by blood lust, the bearded man took another enraptured swing at his weakened opponent, driving his fist through the victim's face with no cause for hesitation.

The death blow was delivered. The victim's stiffly animated legs fell away beneath him, and he dropped to his knees. But it seemed the bearded man was not yet aware of his kill, as his face was stricken with a haughty expression of victory, presenting itself cogently across his moonlike head.

The victim's face bounced on the stone patio, and the light left his eyes. A stream of rich crimson exited from his wounded head; the dark long curls of his hair becoming matted within the blood that poured ceaselessly.

A scream broke out from amongst the crowd, followed by a domino effect of wails and cries. A girl sprinted over to the bearded man and beat his chest with her clenched fists before falling to one knee. She then rolled around the ground in a fit of tears. From her mouth came the semblance of a banshee's wail; a shrill howl that filled every pocket of silence in the evening air.

Although shocking, the scene looked too slapstick to Oscar for any legitimate panic. Everyone now only appeared to be concerned with looking concerned. Only after a long pause did fear erupt in the small black pupils of the aggressor; his expression of hubris, quickly becoming that of a dark terror.

The mourning woman was the first to speak: 'You've killed him?'

She spoke emphatically, unsure where to rest her sight, as her eyes bounded between members of the crowd, as though she asked each of them if her concern was legitimate.

Her facial expression seized, as if a puppeteer pulled at her jowls from the heavens above.

'There is no way this is a thing! There is no way?' she looked around; eyes aghast as a dawn of realisation took hold: 'It's not real!'

She looked to the floor, where the deceased lay. The red blood parted at either side of his entangled mane. The crowd folded outwards as the scarlet river ebbed down the road, entrenching every surface etching on its descent. En masse, the crowd jumped back, as to not have their shoes contaminated by the diluvian scene.

'Oh my God. This is not real!' the girl ripped at her peroxide locks, screaming for someone to call an ambulance, clutching at the burgeoning shoulders of the writhing masses.

It was only now, that the bearded man took his chance to escape. He darted from the scene in a vulpine fashion, bounding over and between the static figures, leaving red droplets of red ichor in his wake.

The shock subsided within the audience, making way for panic. Some wanted to be involved with the proceedings more than others, and those that did; attempted to console the girl, whilst others grouped around the perished man. One, even turned the deceased body over, much to the dismay of others, revealing an expression of painted awe on his pallid face.

There was now, little else for Oscar and Richard to do here, but go inside the pub.

The pair managed to find a table towards the back room on the ground floor, under a television that hung above. There was a bustling queue inside the establishment, which started from the street. Bodies heaved against each other in a bid to see what had taken place outside. The landlord peered through the window at the horde of animated people with a muddled expression. His eyebrow cocked and his bottom lip fastened beneath his top teeth. After rubbing his cheekbones prolifically, he asked what the cause for the houting was, to which a bystander shouted back to him: 'I think someone's been knocked out!' the shrill voice of the bystander cutting through the hubbub.

'Is he on the drive?' the landlord replied.

'Doubt it. I think it happened on the street—the patio.'

A large bead of sweat formed at the top of the landlord's scalp, that ran down his oily skin to greet his perplexed brow.

'So, it's not my problem—yet!' he snorted. 'I'm sure he'll be alright. Do you know who it was?'

'I couldn't tell you,' The bystander said, signing off on the exchange.

The landlord's damp brow reclined as he returned to active duty, shaking his head like a mutt; his spray of sweat seasoning some nearby drinks.

'Wank that,' Oscar thought out loud as he saw those seated and unaware place their lips on the drinks.

'What's that?' Richard asked.

'Doesn't matter. I think he's dead you know,' Oscar whispered to Richard, his eyes growing larger as he leaned into his friend, their noses almost touching.

'You reckon?' said Richard.

'Yes. His head bounced off the ground, did you not see the blood?'

'Yes, not good,' confirmed Richard.

Fred pushed himself into the pair's view, his face a sweltering red. His head resembling a hot air balloon.

'They're forming a queue for me outside, I had to sneak in.'

'Did you see what happened?' asked Oscar abruptly.

'What, the guy outside? It looks like he had a dodgy curry.'

'Did you see his face?' asked Oscar.

Fred pushed his chin into his neck, performing an impression of someone falling over. Warbling his voice: 'He's falling about the shant.'

'Yes, but did you see his face?' Oscar asked again.

'No,' Fred stated, imperatively this time.

'Some bearded guy, proper whacked him and bolted,' said Richard.

'Mate. I just saw him run past,' said Fred enthusiastically.

'What! when you were at the shop?' asked Oscar.

'He ran past me as I was lighting a cig. It was a bearded dude covered in blood. I think it's what's his name from a few years above us...

that Red guy—'.

'Yes, he was absolutely covered in it,' interrupted Oscar.

'No, not red as in red, his name is Red. That's his name. He'll be fucked for good off that. Has he done some serious damage then?'

Richard interjected: 'I can't see him getting away with it. We're not sure if the guy is even alive outside—his jaw was swinging!'

'But there's only charity shops and nonce shops around here, so nothing happens, does it? I doubt anywhere has cameras,' Fred said, before halting his speech; a memory now ignited within him.

'It's like Nisa Local!' he looked to Oscar and Richard with an astonished expression, as though he had just sought out the meaning of life and erupted into song.

'Nisa Local fix your cameras! Nisa Local pay your taxes!'

Fred's melody reigned both Oscar and Richard into chorus; the three of them sung the Nisa Local song.

The boys gorged themselves on the amber nectar of the night, relaying the same tales to one another as they had before, countless times.

Present in the pub, was many of their previous classmates, dotted around the seats, like seeds of memorabilia. Oscar approached them at sporadic intervals throughout the night before returning to his group to speak ill of them. None were afforded liberty, only those most inoffensive were spared, but even they, were labelled as useless.

Oscar and Richard remained at their table for most of the night. Fred was doing the rounds, visiting all who were seated, both young and old. Once he sighted a new group, he used their table corner as a landing strip, shifting his broad shoulders atop it, supported by his comparatively stubby forearms. When appropriately rested on his perch, he would haul his gut onto the table, allowing him to displace any hands, or any gestures of aversion that obstructed him. It was then, his right hand would furl backward; his short fingers doubling back, tickling his wrist. This hand position was known as, 'the claw', and had been aptly named, signaling to the pair that Fred had snorted at the least: two grams.

The atmosphere of the pub was one of hazy jubilance, and Oscar could not recall a time it was this bustling. After reconsidering, perhaps he could. His thoughts were foggy. There was no longer a snap to his ability to converse and his eyelids were heavy. But he knew he must push on, until the merriment of inebriation returned.

He looked at a diminutive man who was sat next to a jukebox, playing the same song on repeat. The man remained hunched over the machine, his shoulders almost level with his ears, dunking another coin into it before the song had even finished.

What a useless idiot, Oscar thought.

He drank to the point there was sufficient delay in his nerve endings, but at the forefront of his mind, the only thing that persisted was the thought of Eva. Although the rampancy of intoxication dampened his trepidation, he still adjusted his hair ad infinitum, pulling on any strand that bowed away from him, yanking it upwards, suspending it within the bulk of his hair.

He asked Richard loudly if he wanted an 'Admiral Bomb', to which Richard obliged. This house special was a mix of Jaeger and something that he couldn't recall.

Oscar stood and readied himself to embark on an expedition of finding Fred. He knew Fred's answer already but was curious to see which of the latest gatherings he may be introduced to.

At first, Oscar struggled to sight the profligate, but after a period, consisting of dodging elbows and a frequent apology, he saw him through a window outside the main entrance. He peered through the foggy glass, out to the dusk. Fred's ruddy cheeks shone a vibrant pink against the dark canvas behind him, illuminated by the lambent orange flame of his cigarette. Seated below Fred were three women who looked to be increasingly weathered from left to right. Oscar sighed, rapping on the glass with his knuckle.

He knocked once, then twice, then thrice. Fred's eyes caught Oscar's, and the drunk's cigarette looked like a sparkler whizzing through the darkening atmosphere. The women were also alerted to Oscar's presence when Fred roared something behind the glass, waving his hands about frantically, turning his torso side to side dramatically. Oscar could only imagine what these words were.

He gestured a drinking motion to Fred, wiping the condensation away from the glass with the cuff of his free arm.

Fred motioned to his watch, to which Oscar proffered a sardonic smirk.

Oscar looked around the pub as he leant on the bar with his ribcage, barely enough space for both of his shoulders to exist on the same plane as his head. When his arm broke free, he flitted it between coiling his hair round his finger and adjusting his brittle watch. He took extra care not to meet the gaze of anyone he may know, or may know him. It was a legitimate fear of his; that any of these suspecting figures may strike up a conversation with him and that they might also be content, standing amidst the air of his disappointment. He saw many girls he knew who were once young and had now burgeoned into fledgling women. He was cautious not to ogle at them, forcing himself to back down against his drunken inhibitions.

He returned to the table, brushing from him a patch of syrupy boozed that covered his thigh. He gave Richard the glass the bartender's finger had slipped into after pouring; Richard wouldn't care.

'You're alright here, aren't you? I'm going to hunt down Fred. Are you staying at mine still, yeah?'

'I will do, I'm going to ring Fran in a sec. I might get something to eat,' Richard swung on his seat as though it were part of a carousel, looking up at Oscar aimlessly.

'You're a bit of a weapon aren't you,' Oscar said, before departing.

He found Fred still at his dwelling, and to Oscar's surprise, the faces of the women remained coy, and Fred's audience had grown. Oscar tapped the back of the court jester's neck, handing him his physick.

Fred leaned backwards and breathed huskily on Oscar's neck.

'I love you bro, fuck all these, they don't mean anything to me mate. They're not the same; they're not like us. They don't know each other like we do. It's just me and you mate. It always is and it always has been.'

Oscar's toes curled and he forced his nails into his hands. Through gritted teeth he returned a show of affection to his friend, clasping him on the shoulder. He then walked briskly back inside, whipping his head over his shoulder to watch his friend reintroduce himself to his subjects. As Fred swayed, his jeans fell to his kneecaps. But with the drunk's free hand, he managed to scoop them up before they arrived at his ankles.

Oscar could still hear Fred's roars as he entered the building; the drunk's only recourse of silence was when his glass slapped against his chapped lips or chinked against his unbrushed teeth. Oscar knew that Fred must now be left to his own affairs for the duration.

'His pants are riding up his arse again,' said Oscar, as he sat himself next to a cackling Richard, pushing against his leg to create room.

A moment of silence ensued.

'Insane earlier innit,' said Oscar, his eyes darting from the bar to the window.

'Yeah, I'm surprised they haven't shut this place down,' said Richard

'I've not heard an ambulance arrive.'

'It definitely came, I saw it outside when I went to the toilet,' Richard clarified.

'I need a piss dude, give me a sec.'

Richard pointed across the bar. 'I've just seen Josh anyway; I'm going to have to go over and say hello.'

Oscar stood, checking that both his phone and wallet were in their respective pockets.

'Oh yeah, Josh? Say hello to him for me. I'd love to have a chat with him.'

Richard rolled his eyes laconically.

Oscar could never remember where the toilets were in this place. They had not moved, but the swaying crowd served to disorientate him. He pushed against the milling bodies, asking people politely to make way for him, and other times, he took advantage of their delirious state, pushing them aside. He found the staircase at the back end of the establishment.

The crowds opened, revealing a wide berth of claggy black steps that were laden in ichor. The stench of urine was apparent. He yanked his boots up each step in a bid to not cover his soles in the viscosity of hooch.

He plucked his phone from his jeans and with some effort punched his passcode in wrong a total of three times. He stopped on the stairs and leant against the banister on his left, careful not to touch it with anything but his sleeve.

'The fuck,' he muttered to himself, squinting at the subject of his dismay; this phone was nothing but a thorn in his side when he needed it most.

He took a generous look up the stairs to gauge the rest of his journey. But saw, stood before him: Eva. She looked at him somewhat amusingly, being so generous as to allow him to see the corners of her curled mouth and the dimples on her spheral cheeks.

She stood on the step that preceded the top of the stairs. The pair stood eye to eye. Her palladium locks gave way to the unblemished perfection of her features; the crowning jewels of which, were her large crystalline blue-green eyes. They hummed with gentle mystery, and her silver lips spoke mortal words to him.

'Hey.'

She wore a dumpy black cardigan, of which the sleeves hung delicately over her small wrists, that coiled round her folded arms. She was wearing all black, like Oscar, but with a rose gold necklace that hung a short distance from her sweetheart neckline.

There was little time for Oscar to form a neurotic response, and he settled with common decency instead: 'How's it going, you good?'

He tried to stop his arms from phrasing the question for him and dunked his phone back into his pocket, grabbing the banister. He placed his free hand on his hip, only to realise he now resembled a tea pot. He hoisted his hand behind him, clasping the back of his glistening neck.

The dim lights hid his flushed cheeks, forming a temporary alliance with him. A taut moment passed; he was unsure if Eva was at a loss for words or if she was reveling in his discomfort. He was convinced, however, that regardless of his fanaticism, he appeared well put together. He tongued what remained of his chewing gum, pushing it to the back of his mouth, securing it behind his molars and cocked his head toward his left ear.

Eva proffered a warm smile, spelling the end of their exchange as she walked down the steps past him, her arms still folded.

A tide of unease overcame him. He knew it melodramatic, but he wished to kill himself.

Oscar tried again, fueled by his unhinged descent.

'I think we went to college with each other, you know?'

'High Beaumont?' she asked. Her eyes were now a dizzying blue, their verdant embellishments abandoned under the light.

'That's the one... I really like your nails,' said Oscar, looking to her hands desperately.

'Oh, thank you,' she did not smile but ran a long-nailed finger through a loose strand of hair that fell before her winsome ear.

Oscar's head became hot and sweat encroached upon his hairline to thwart him. He smiled meaningfully at her.

'I'll catch you in a bit.'

She replied courteously, 'sure,' and completed her descent down the gummed steps. He turned and failed to restrain a hushed curse escaping his lips. He retrieved his phone from his pocket and squeezed upon it so tightly that his knuckles turned a ghostly white. This made him feel feint, so he eased his grip, instead digging his nails into his screen. His screen fractured; a splinter of willow glass shot from it and hit him in the chin. He thought a passersby might have seen this, so he stepped down to the ground floor, before remembering he needed the toilet.

Richard was still not present on Oscar's return, but Oscar sighted him under a set of wooden beams afar, making merriment with Josh and his brigade. He placed himself down on the seat and tapped his empty glass with his nails. Now aware that Eva was in the vicinity, he was careful to not be sighted alone by her. He discreetly looked over the busy interior for more than the thousandth time this evening but could not sight where she was; doubting if she was even present. Maybe she had already left, he thought. She was wearing her cardigan, perhaps she was readying herself to leave? She was heading back from the toilets after all. It was a convincing case he presented to himself.

A green envy rose within him. he did not want anyone to look at her. He did not want anyone to know her. He did not want anyone to revel in her audience. He prayed she did not appear to him as she appeared to all else. The starlet amongst the dross; he would give every lifetime for her, tenfold, twentyfold, until the planet was naught more than a hostile crater in a sea of dead stars. He would accept this damned fate, or any fate for that matter, so long as he were to have her.

His infatuation became so overbearing, he could not remember what she looked like. In memory, her profile only appeared to him as a crescent moon with a lunar white surface, shimmering radiantly in all directions. If you were to ask of him to place her features, or to sketch her face, he would not be able to do so. This feeling was so intense it made him sick; he wished to leave.

He did not want to know what audience the night held for her and could not bring himself to bear witness to any. He was not equipped to strike up another conversation with her and knew he must retreat to his room to envisage new machinations.

He waded over the mire of shoes to Richard and told him that he was to depart shortly.

'Are you getting a lift back with Fran, or are you coming with me?'

'I'll probably go back with Fran,' said Richard.

'Of course,' Oscar said pedantically, before reattuning his sentiment, 'Okay, no worries. Have you seen Fred?'

'Yeh, I think he's outside still, he's—'.

As Richard was speaking, Oscar sighted a previous acquaintance from school approach him through the mob. The figure's head was bobbing under the waves of bodies.

'Oscar how are you, bro?'

Ellis had set upon him, at a time marred with much disdain.

Oscar did his best impression of a reasonable human being.

'Yo! I won't keep you because I'm about to shoot. Are you good though?'

He turned his body away from the nuisance, keeping his head cocked towards the invader, hoping he would sense his scorn.

'So good brother! Work is going great, I'm so glad I didn't go to college; I'm working construction at the minute.'

'Oh, awesome stuff. Happy for you dude,' replied Oscar flatly.

Ellis seemed to be hell-bent on keeping contact with his wandering eyes.

'I manage quite a few people now. I've got my own thing going for me. Are you still in Kellwell? It's a great town to go out in, but you don't really want to stay here, do you? You need to get out whilst you can. That's what I think—'.

Oscar's thoughts blurted out to him, but they remained trapped beneath his tongue. He stared at Ellis' mousey face with an expression devoid of any sentiment.

'That's impressive. Owning a construction company at nineteen? I've got to be honest with you, I'm just bumming it at the minute.'

'So, it's sort of—well, it's family based originally, but I've taken the reigns in the last year or so.'

Oscar normally would humor such a dunce, but he was tired, and drunk, and felt like a victim. So instead, he chose to take Ellis' lacking display of self-awareness as one of abject tedium.

'Best of luck to you anyway. Fingers crossed!' Oscar shouted, swiftly rotating his head before he could see the converser's reaction, departing out the side door.

Outside, the milling bodies of the dejected lined the street; many stumbling, but none falling. How unamusing, Oscar thought. He strutted past them briskly, whipping his hand through his hair as he made his way back through the town. The din of the pub faded into a backdrop of darkness. The night air was clammy and the stars that hung above did little to impress.

PART ONE - INFATUATION

CHAPTER THREE

THE DATE

Oscar launched his phone against his bedroom wall. The device bounced back landing just before his feet. He did it once again; this time, it fell abruptly to the base of the wall.

He ran up to it and hoofed it with his heel. The print of his boot marking the cream wallpaper.

He retrieved his phone, and his face was glum. He stood in darkness and looked about. Even amidst the cast shadows, he could see whisps of dust creeping from under his furniture. He considered hoovering them up, but not with any seriousness, or right now.

He dressed down to his boxers and stretched his arms forth in the muggy heat. A bitterness still gripped his being and he had hoped by shedding his clothes he would alleviate himself of such a burden. He refused to open the window; the thought of an allergy attack at the early hours of the morning was unbearable.

He launched his phone at the wall once more, viciously. A loud cracking noise tolled as it struck. The skeletal frame of the phone finally shattering, succumbing to its punishment. The phone lay dead on the floor with large cracks across it resembling a mosaic. He tried to turn it on, but his monolith of information was no more. He acted annoyed at this discovery, as if this was not his intent. He pressed on the screen gently, peering at it with wide eyes.

He searched for his laptop, failing to find it at first, but after rummaging around in the darkness, he sighted it poking out from under a jumbled pile of clothes.

He retrieved it and kicked the clothes back in a pile, sweating profusely. The light of the laptop screen illuminated his belly and his white pants. He jumped on top of his bed with it clutched between his arms, hoping to crash through his mattress into the ground floor below; creating a scene so dire, it would erase the night from his mind. He thought how painful crashing through a floor might be. But of course, he did not have any choice in this theoretical matter and landed on his bed awkwardly; the springs of the mattress only emitting a creaking sigh upon impact. He kicked the sheets from his legs, which coiled around him like hot whips, and lay still for a moment looking at the bright screen, unable to conjure the will to enter his password.

He got up from his short-lived rest and sprinted downstairs to the kitchen. He ripped a half full bottle of squash out from the cupboard and poured its contents into the sink, choosing instead to pump it full of tap water. He necked from the bottle, guzzling at the water as it splashed over the bottle rim onto his nipples, making him jump in surprise. He filled the bottle back to the brim and shot back upstairs, positioning it unsteadily on the carpet. He jumped back into his bed and sprawled out across it, reacquiring the laptop, balancing it on his gut.

He was drunker than he had anticipated, and the darkness of the room began to sour his comfortability rather than placate it. When still, the room writhed and twisted, making it difficult for him to think of anything else but his lack of sobriety. He did not want to be sick; being sick would ruin the following day, and perhaps the one after as well.

The saliva in his mouth turned hot, a feeling all too familiar. He glugged again from the bottle and swallowed down his spit repeatedly. The more that came from his glands; with greater intensity did he swallow, with added vehemence and deliberation at each gulp.

When the wave of sickness subsided, he considered masturbating, thinking again of Eva. He resisted; she didn't deserve that. He logged on to his laptop and was met by the Windows home screen. He sat up and put the device in front of his crossed legs, looking intently at the glowing screen. He opened a browser and tried to log in to Facebook, almost throwing the laptop off his bed when it did not log him in automatically. In umbrage, he went through the rigmarole of recovering his password and his email address before the site let him in. He typed Eva's full name into the search bar, and to his bemusement they were already friends.

He opened her profile and looked at the chat box at the side of the page, eyeing her availability icon with some distress. She was inactive currently. In her profile picture she wore a full face of makeup accompanied by one of her friends. Her banner picture was a sunset vista with her bare feet in frame. He checked the time at the bottom right of the screen, which read, 01:23. It was late; maybe too late. He overrode his hardwiring and began to hammer at his musty keyboard. What he typed, at first was far too arid and could be misconstrued too easily over the medium of text. He tried again, glossing over the letters which rose and fell before him in his stupor, deciding upon the only words that didn't pain him.

OSCAR
'Guess who'

He waited for some time. His foot started to tingle, and he kept his head aloft in the palm of his hand, with his arm balancing restlessly on top of his kneecap. Precisely four minutes later, Eva's availability icon turned green. When he saw this, he almost slammed down the lid of his laptop, nearly adding it to the scrapyard of tech he was starting to accrue.

Eva read the message.
He waited. Nothing.

EVA
'Who? Hahaha'

It was done; in Oscar's mind, finished. The cards had been dealt, the stars had aligned, and the fat lady had sung. He feigned busyness for two minutes before replying.

OSCAR
'Your favourite. Why are you up at this hour?'

The message was received, but nothing was returned.

OSCAR
'We should go out sometime'

EVA
'I've only spoken to you once lol'

OSCAR
'It's enough for me to know'

EVA
'Know what?'

OSCAR
'That you're boring. But I'd like to give you a second chance.'

EVA
'Looool'

Oscar remained composed, staring at the screen discerningly.

EVA
'When?'

OSCAR
'Tomorrow. You live in Kellwell?'

EVA
'In Hawthorne Gardens'

OSCAR
'Sweet, I'll meet you there. Do you fancy going to the fair on the green?'

EVA
'Oh, is it on tomorrow?'

OSCAR
'Tis'

EVA
'Okay, I'll text you when I'm ready. Are you thinking like seven?'

OSCAR
'Seven thirty. My phone is broken so I'll just meet you outside yours'

EVA
'Lol okay. But go down the road a bit, do not wait outside mine. I'll meet you at the bench at the bottom of my road. Do you know which one I mean?'

OSCAR
'No. But I'll find it. If I'm not there, assume I've found someone else to go with.'

EVA
'I'm going to bed now, night.'

OSCAR
'Nanight x'

He regretted putting the kiss, though he was suffering from an intense bout of infatuation, so quickly forgave himself; overjoyed by the merits of his discourse. He looked down to see an outline crop up from his boxers. He relieved himself and placed his laptop down beside his bed carefully and fell asleep.

He awoke the next day at eleven o' clock, forgetting almost entirely the events of the night before apart from those which pertained to Eva. He slapped himself across his aching skull, peering over his covers to his shattered phone. He recovered his laptop from beside him and flipped it open. Facebook was still open, and he'd received a message from Richard an hour ago. His friend had asked if he was alright, stating that he had tried to ring multiple times to no avail. Before Oscar could reply, Richard messaged again.

RICHARD
'That guy died you know, they mentioned it on the local news this morning'

Oscar hit the video call button, reliving the memories of the night in a patchwork fashion. His call was immediately answered; Richard's pimples and imperfections came into obscure view as his head flooded the screen.
'What the fuck are you on?'
'I've had to go on my laptop, my phone broke. I think the charger fucked it.'
'Should have ordered a new one.'

'Yeah, yeah,' Oscar conceded. 'He died?'

'Fran told me this morning; it came up on the news.'

Oscar let his head flop back onto his pillow; the weight of his skull overpowering his neck.

'Who was it who died, did they say?'

'No, they didn't give a name. Fran said he was registered as dead on arrival.'

'Does dead on arrival mean dead at the hospital?' asked Oscar.

'I think so.'

'Does Fran know who it was?'

Oscar rubbed at the point of his nose aggressively.

'She said they're still looking for him.'

'Ah—that's insane! Do you understand how mental that is?'

Oscar sniffed illimitably as the morning pollen made its way down the chimney.

'But they not know it's Red, right?'

'I don't have a clue. She said they were asking for people to come forward.'

Oscar frowned.

'I guess someone has already come forward. There was a whole crowd of people who saw it? Wait, so hold on. A guy who was covered in blood, running through town somehow made it to a place of hiding, and wasn't caught on camera or stopped by anyone?' Oscar reevaluated what he said. 'Well, I suppose no one is going to stop him, actually.'

'Yeah, but maybe Fred was right? No cameras,' said Richard idly.

Oscar pursued the subject, pretending to understand the innerworkings of law enforcement.

'There's just no way though, is there? They should have enough on him already.'

'Maybe?' Richard's face froze in motion as he spoke, the connection interrupting.

'Do you know what happened to Fred?' asked Oscar.

'No, I just left him, doubt he's even slept yet.'

'Waste of time.'

'Yeah', agreed Richard resoundingly. 'Did you read my message about tonight? Do you want to come round?'

A series of horrific noises alerted Oscar to his peripheral. The cacophonous sound could only be likened to an Imp from an infernal realm screeching and clawing from within his bedroom wall.

'Can you hear this shit?' Oscar tried to quell his concern by laughing nervously.

'Yeah!' Richard snorted. 'What the fuck was that?'

Oscar sprung from his bed, almost knocking his laptop to the floor, his right ear pricked. He spun the laptop round so that Richard had a view of him. At least if he was to be savaged by a strange creature, it would be caught on camera.

Oscar cautiously mouthed the words 'what the hell,' as he squinted vexingly at the fireplace. He crouched slightly, but not so it was noticeable to Richard who was now ogling Oscar's movements with much excitement and equal parts disbelief. He grabbed the waistband of his boxers and yanked them down slightly. He did not wish for his pants to be riding higher than his belly button in his final moments.

The startling noises came once again from the wall. It was now clear that the sounds were coming from inside the fireplace; something must have fallen into it. His theory was soon confirmed, as a dull thud sounded from within the hearth, and a rampant squawking noised. Oscar craned his head back towards the screen, casting an eye to Richard. Richard's head appearing giant and his body small and distant. If Oscar was not so troubled, he would have laughed at the perspective of Richard's massive head. His friend looked back at him confused, struggling with the lack of clarity from the speakers.

'Have you found out what it—is?' asked Richard.

Oscar exhaled the words. 'It's a bird, for fuck's sake.'

Richard's mouth opened involuntarily, saliva spraying across his camera as he snickered.

'Just open your window and it should fly out'

'But it's just been up the fucking chimney hasn't it and that means it's covered in shit. If I let it out it will cover my room in shit.'

Richard's chortling did little to placate him. 'No, no. It won't, just open the window.'

'I can't just let it out, can I? Because the fireplace is barred by fucking planks.'

'Wank that,' agreed Richard.

'I might just leave it in there, I'm not lying.'

The clucking cries from the hearth intensified.

The connection of the call faltered on Richard's end again, freezing his face in an expression of much contemplation. His words though, were still ever-present.

'You can't l just leave it; it might have broken a wing. You're not going to leave a dead bird for your Mum to get back to, are you?'

'I can, I keep loads in the attic.'

'Is Eva up there?' asked Richard.

'Funny you should mention that I think I'm seeing her later,' Oscar said in contentment, over the dying squawks in the background. 'I think we might be going to the fair.'

'How did you manage that?' asked Richard.

'Messaged her. I'll let you know if she bails—or I might just kill myself.'

'Shall we just deal with this though, first?'

'Yarp,' confirmed Oscar.

He moved over to the fireplace and shuddered, goosebumps breaking out across his white back. 'I think what I'm going to do, is kick the wood a bit to see if it flies back up,' he looked back to the screen where Richard's avatar persisted. 'I'm stalling.'

'You are,' Richard concurred.

He kneeled and placed his hands on the rotten wood that barred both his entry, and the bird's escape.

'No. I'm getting gloves; this is just insane behaviour.'

He ran across the room scavenging for his laptop charger, only to find it on the top shelf. He made sure Richard's avatar was plugged in, and darted downstairs, grabbing a pair of his mother's bright yellow gloves before returning.

'Captain Underpants,' Oscar said, jigging performatively to Richard in his new attire, spinning round and jutting his butt out.

'I wish your Mum walked into that.'

Oscar returned to the fireplace and broke away the wood that was loosely nailed to the plinth and the corbel above.

'Do you think there's woodworm in here, on these planks?'

'Could be,' Richard laughed.

Oscar looked back at him, raising a black eyebrow.

'I'm joking,' said Richard laconically.

Oscar placed his foot to the left of the fireplace, securely fastening his hands round the wood; once a suitable grip was actioned, he pulled at them with intent. The continued flurry of squawks was encouragement enough that they were coming loose. The planks fractured in the middle, making it difficult to get a clean break, and he was now concerned by the protruding rusty nails that gleamed a dark iron colour.

'I'm going to get tetanus bro,' said Oscar sincerely.

'You're not.'

He yanked with all his might at the wooden planks, and they loosened, beginning to break away from the hearth. He was committed to any result at this point and arched his back against his bed, tugging at the wood until jewels of sweat ran from his brow.

'Fuck—I haven't opened my window!' leaving his operation fleetingly, he pushed up the window until it jammed. He returned and laboriously wrenched at the planks until they broke away. He dropped them to the floor and hopped back against his bed, eyeing the black opening suspiciously.

To Oscar's surprise and relief, the bird did not fly out from the chasm. He leaned closer, his eyes appearing as two giant white marbles in the darkness. He could see the pigeon's grey form in the depths.

'Yup, it's a pigeon'.

'Yup,' replied Richard in unison.

Oscar offered his yellow glove to the pigeon, hoping that this action would somehow transcend the communication barrier, causing the pigeon to take his lead.

'I might have to pick it up, I think its wings are broken? Or one of them, I guess.'

He observed the partial form of the bird but could not see its full structure. Its wings were shrouded in a shadowy backdrop, as though the pigeon was adamantly hiding from him. He moved his face closer to the hearth.

He was met by a deafening squawk, and the pigeon shot out from the depths, revealing its freakishly lengthy wingspan. The contaminated vessel sailed through the air, glancing Oscar's pale face with its claw as it passed.

Oscar reeled in shock and fell to the carpet, writhing on the floor, imitating the actions of one who been grazed on the cheek by a broadsword. All the while, a hysterical roar came from his laptop speakers.

'I actually think I've been poisoned,' Oscar held his face in contempt, looking about the floor, as though a cure might be found in the recesses of the carpet.

'Is it gone?' asked Oscar, remaining on the floor.

'It went out of the window, it's a good job you remembered to open it,' Richard said, wiping a welling tear from his eye.

'I've got some weird disease now. This is all your fault; I'd have left it in there! Fuck's sake man.'

'That was all a bit strange,' Richard said, scrunching his nose in bemusement.

'I would have preferred to get rocked by that Red guy; rather than die slowly from pigeon scratch,' Oscar stood up, clad still, in his pants and gloves; now with three red scratch marks under his right eye.

He continued his monologue.

'Pigeons are useless, aren't they? They're basically the equivalent to wasps. What are they good for? What are wasps good for?'

He looked directly into Richard's pixelated eyes. 'And most importantly, what are you good for, you jammy little cunt.'

Richard's silence gave way to a pearly smile, revealing his nacre teeth.

Oscar marched over to the window, slamming it shut. He stood on his tiptoes to eye the blind spots at each side of him shielded by the window frame. The last thing he wanted was for the carnaptious grey devil to be waiting for him the next time he arrived here.

'I am going to have to resist researching what diseases pigeons carry,' he sighed.

He sensed Richard was at his wit's end. Either that, or the connection had been severed.

'Don't research anything—I'll speak to you in a bit. Let me know if it doesn't end up happening later,' said Richard.

'Okay dude, I'll let you know. I can always do something tomorrow,' replied Oscar.

'Catch you later.'

'In a bit.'

Oscar stood alone; a muted light shined on him through the window. After a moment's grace, he ripped his gloves off and dumped them in the wash basket, shoving them all the way to the bottom. He took off his boxer shorts and jumped under the shower, turning it to a medium heat.

Once washed and ready, he stood over the kitchen sink, toying with the decision to eat or not. His logic was purely derived from a hope, he would kiss Eva later. He also somewhat enjoyed the dehydration of a hangover. The look of gauntness he felt in his face following a shindig was pleasing to behold. He rifled through the contents of kitchen cupboards, swearing he had left a tub of gum somewhere within its depths. He found his prize behind an empty box of cereal and poured the gum into his mouth, saving three pieces for later.

He exited the kitchen and caught himself in the dining room mirror. He was fond of the bird scratches. Even after cleaning himself intensely, they remained a bright crimson. He thought these cuts might be used as a fine talking point, even if they were to kill him.

He made it to the living room, shirking off the allure of the mirror and picked up a leftover can of ale; cracked it open and indulged. He set himself a limit of four cans. That way, he would not have to go to the toilet an unforeseen number of times in the evening but would benefit from an alcoholic conviction.

After finishing the beers too quickly, he set an alarm on his phone and settled onto the sofa. He closed his eyes, hoping his thoughts would cease. But alas, his mind could not rest. He thought of cascading rivers and rolling hills but was unable to coax himself to sleep over the helpless tapping of his foot.

He considered pulling out of the date; he could always make an excuse; an ignoble forte of his. However, he knew this would lead to a melancholic episode that might be crippling. His back was against the wall, and there was little he could do. He weaved a tangle of ruminations, arriving at a single conclusion; the events of the night would take place, if he were to be there or not, therefore, he should be there. This logic would buy him enough respite to make it out of the house later in good spirits. He hoped it would provide him ample assurance throughout the evening too, but knew, in his heart, this was not one of his strongest resolutions.

He locked up and departed from the house on the hill at six o' clock, nursing a growing concern that he would not be able to find Eva's home, or even the estate in which she lived. It was of course not possible for him to make such a blunder, as Oscar had been to Hawthorne Gardens in his developmental years. One of his school friends had lived there; it was at the more modest end of Kellwell.

He headed through the pleasantly warm town; the sky was a golden blue, and the breeze carried the aroma of his youth from the park. A scent of freshly cut grass was eminent above all else, reminding him of his allergies, for which he had forgotten his medication. He stopped at the shop on the town's corner. The price of the tablets was exorbitant; going forward he would have to rely on his mother's money as the first line of defence against pollen. From the shop shelves, he also grabbed more chewing gum, and when outside, loaded them up in his mouth like sweets.

He made it to the bench at the bottom of Eva's road in good time. There was no other bench present here, so this one seemed fitting. He was desperately early and headed back down the road, stowing himself behind the dingy corner shop he frequented. From here, he could not be sighted by passing drivers, but had a keen view of the bench through the trees.

He checked his phone; the time was only twenty past six. He knew he would be early but could never account for just how early he would be. He was baffled that people could be so relaxed about lateness. As if lifely importance was not placed on an event in question. For a meeting to exist, all involved must pool their time into a ceaseless pit, and arriving late—whether it be a friend, family member, or whoever, implies that the latecomer believes that the laurels must go to them, and not those in attendance. He thought it the height of vanity. What could be so important that one could not be on time for?

His face turned a flustered red, and he thought to visit his childhood home. It lay a short distance up from the shop, in the opposite direction of Eva's road. He embarked in this direction for one minute but could not bring himself to abandon his post entirely. As, if any unforeseen circumstances were to occur, he doubted his ability to return to the bench before seven o' clock. He spied the bench again through the gap between the trees, wondering if Eva could see the bench from her window.

He thought there might not be anything more tragic to the eye than an admirer sat on a bench, a short distance from their darling's house, only to be caught awaiting their presence an hour early. The destituteness one must find themselves in to be caught doing this, alarmed Oscar.

The sky above was now a calm violet, and the cars passed by the shop more frequently. What if he was to be sighted behind the trees? he thought. Perhaps the onlooker would know Eva; living close by to her themselves, telling her of a stalker that waited for her near the end of her road in a copse.

Oscar entered the shop and went to the back fridge. He pulled a large bottle of beer from the cabinet and counted his change prudently, before purchasing it.

The shop bell sounded as he left, and he turned the corner to face the bench. He sighted a silver car pulling into a drive opposite it. He could not make out what the car was, nor was this important to him, but it looked well used. The driver's door popped open, and a figure of some proportion leant out of it donned in a grey hooded top.

The figure stretched himself from the car. And although Oscar was some distance away, he managed to catch a glimpse of the man's side profile, which made Oscar increasingly suspicious; the figure's hulking build and profile resembled the escapee from last night.

The figure entered the bungalow. There were no other cars parked in the drive, and it was scarcely large enough for the silver car alone. Once the man had disappeared into the house, the blinds were drawn, and lights remained off. Oscar was mystified, his mouth remaining round his bottle of beer; his head following its slow trajectory forth as he prized the bottle from his lips. Upon reflection, he conceded that he may be wrong; declaring that this sighting could well be a trick of the dimming light, or a misinformed impression. Yet, he had not drunk enough to have such an uninformed take, surely?

He finished his beer, retreating to the verdant thicket behind the shop. He dropped the empty bottle into the greenery and kicked a boscage of shrubs over it. He urinated on it, heedful to not spray his trousers as he did. He considered asking Eva about Red, but ultimately thought it was best to not draw the attention away from him. Although, it may act as a point of interest, so he declared to himself he would feel out the meeting first.

He rehearsed his opening line a multitude of times, imitating Eva's reaction to it in several ways. It was quarter past the hour of seven, and he made an educated guess that between ten and five minutes early was socially acceptable, and if Eva was to see him at this time, it would not dissuade her interest.

He hastily walked back up the road, eyeing the potential home of Red. Still, the curtains remained drawn, and the lights remained off. He sat down on the bench, facing the road awkwardly. He cupped his cheeks in his hands and arced his head down so far that his shoulders almost met his chest, becoming oblivious to all outside a five-foot vicinity of him.

'How long have you been here?'

The sweet voice came from behind his right ear.

'Like five minutes, maybe?' answered Oscar. He still faced the empty road, unwilling to turn.

'You're a liar,' she laughed.

'I am, you're right. More like fifteen.'

'I could see you here from my window!'

'I thought you could.'

Oscar turned round with a carefully placed smile upon him to see Eva's annular face. Two large resplendent hoops hung from her ears at either side, and her expression resembled that of a cat's; a cat that had just brought its owner a dead mouse.

Oscar climbed to his feet and ruffled her hair gently, to which he regretted instantly.

'Thanks,' said Eva.

She was wearing an outfit like the one she wore the previous night, but he could not tell if it was the same, or something akin to it. The only remarkable difference being, she now wore a sky-blue top underneath her black cardigan with a rose gold filigree pendant attached to her necklace. It was pretty, she was, intensely pretty.

It was at this moment, the dawning of his predicament set in. He must now entertain her all the way to the fair and then some.

She looked at him with entreating eyes.

'Shall we?' Oscar said, motioning his hand in front of him, placing it abruptly back into his pocket, after leaving it hanging a moment too long. Eva walked to his flank, allowing him to lead the way.

'It's mental that you haven't got a phone. I've never been with anyone who doesn't have a phone,' said Eva.

'Been with?' Oscar smirked.

She slapped his arm preciously: 'Shut up!'

'Why did you not talk to me at college? Why are you only doing this now?'

'Honestly, I never saw you at college. I was there to do a job and get my head down. I screwed up at school and had to resit the year; they didn't let me resit at Kelwell's.'

'I saw you eating alone a few times.'

'I must have been waiting for someone.'

Eva smiled.

'Have you been to the fair before?' asked Oscar.

'Yeah! Me and Layla went last year, it's okay. It's not the best, but we normally go anyway. There's fuck all to do in Kellwell isn't there?'

'Layla?' Oscar asked.

'Layla is the one in my profile pic.'

Oscar brought up the picture in his mind's eye. She looked like trouble; they all did. He did his best impression of someone whose life depended on being interested in Eva's answer.

'Ah!'

'Layla's great! She's just a great friend, she was my only proper friend at college. I do have other friends who went but she's the one that's always been there for me.'

Oscar was in awe of her eyes, the purview of which was devastating.

The pair walked to the bottom of the hill. The destination lay on the Burgage, at the top of their ascent.

'Did you hear about the guy who got killed last night?' asked Eva.

'I did,' Oscar answered, solemnly.

'You've got to be an actual scum bag, haven't you? Like, the actual worst person. How can you live with yourself after doing something like that?'

Eva looked up at him expectingly.

'It's not ideal is it,' said Oscar.

'Oscar. He's dead.' She looked as though she was trying to hold back a confused laugh. 'The guy is fully dead, I think it's a bit worse than not ideal, isn't it?'

'I'm messing,' replied Oscar, curtly. 'He lives near you I think?'

'What! The guy who did it?' Eva shouted, aghast.

'I think he's a few years older than us. It's that Red guy; I saw him go into a bungalow across from your road.' Oscar pointed in a rounda-

Lilies Of The Damned

bout direction; through the sleeping houses they had passed by.

'You're joking! Oh my God. He does! He lives down the road.'

Oscar nodded convincingly, as though he had just solved the case.

'Why has he not been locked up? Is he still about? How do you know it's him!'

The barrage of questions was insufferable, but at the least, he was glad the conversation was riveting enough that it held her attention, even if he was not the focal point.

Eva went on: 'Has no one reported it?'

'They must have, there were load of witnesses. I don't know if he's on bail, I'm not sure how it works being honest with you,' answered Oscar.

'No, I don't think that's how it works. I think he would be held at a police station. Are you sure it's him? Maybe you're wrong?'

'It's him,' said Oscar.

'We'll see, I'm not convinced,' Eva said, casting her eyes away from him.

'Shall I win you a teddy?' Oscar asked, with a smile.

'I hate teddy bears. You can try, though!' her laugh sounded like a waterfall of pennies.

'I was thinking of winning you a fish, actually,' Oscar retorted.

'I'd feed it to my lizard.'

Oscar snorted, mucous nearly streaming from his nose.

'I fucking love lizards—when I was a kid, I used to draw them all the time. Is it a Leopard Gecko? My parents never let me have one of those.'

'Mine is so cute, I love him.'

'No way! So, it is a leopard gecko?'

'Yeah,' said Eva. She gazed into the distance distractedly, to the encroaching lights and humming sound of the fair.

'Do you get him out the cage much?'

'I feed him crickets; the cage is in my room'.

'You crazy girl. It's a good job you're nice to look at'.

Eva looked back at Oscar, squinting. Her eyelids did little to enclose

53

the giant jadeite orbs which filled her face.

'I can't tell if you even like me?'

'You're okay,' said Oscar.

'What happened to your face?' Eva asked, as she ran her light finger down his cheek, her nail grazing his flesh delicately.

'A cat did that?'

'Close, a bear.'

'Do you take anything seriously?'

'It was a bird, I rescued it from my chimney earlier, and it clawed my face on escape. Can you believe that?'

A streetlight turned on above them.

'Do you know what? I can believe that.'

'Shit innit,' Oscar said, running his hand across his face. The amber glow lit up his features as dusk ensued overhead.

'Aw. I prefer animals to humans; they never do anything wrong.'

'If you don't count savaging each other as wrong,' said Oscar.

'It's their nature,' replied Eva.

The courter and his darling set foot on the green of the Burgage. Ahead of them, was a sight of sickly splendor.

They drank from the sights and sounds of the fair. A rusted crimson tower climbed high above them, emitting a stench of iron. Its frame raucously creaking from the weight of the fairgoers that swung from it across the dying skies of the evening. They swung hopelessly, cheering and crying out for more of the same.

Stalls: selling blue candy floss, rainbow swirls, candy apples and hot dogs, were present, owned by men who had once attended this show of plastic opulence in wonderment themselves.

The neon glows of the stalls separated them from their metal counterparts. Some had shooting ranges lined with plushies of stuffed animals, crowned by a large brown bear that sat upright in the middle of the display, its ears unfurled, and its stitching brimming in hues of ochre. Propped up, and plump, a king amongst its subjects.

'I'm going to win that,' said Oscar.

Eva wasn't listening, her eyes were glazed over with the shimmering display.

'Doughnuts!' she cried.

'I believe that's what they're called,' said Oscar.

'Shut up! Do you like them?' asked Eva.

'I do. The proper battered sugary ones.'

Eva licked her lips and Oscar made sure his crotch was appropriately adjusted.

'I'll get you one if you want?'

Eva replied enthusiastically: 'No! Shall we share one? They are quite big, aren't they?'

'You can have one to yourself, it's not a big deal'.

Eva looked at her glaring surroundings with a furrowed silver brow.

'I'll grab one, and we can share it,' clarified Oscar.

'Okay, do you want some money for it?'

'No, no.'

Oscar purchased the frosted doughnut and presented it to her in a paper bag.

Eva's face lit up with childlike joy; her pearl white teeth protruding from her top lip. In guile, Oscar slid another piece of gum into his mouth.

'I'll not have a lot of it,' she said, raising the bag to her nose.

'You can have what you want, it's yours.'

'You said it was to share!' squealed Eva.

'I'll try some,' said Oscar.

Eva took a bite from the doughnut; the powder covered her lips and she giggled.

'These ones are so good, aren't they?'

'I'll let you know, once you've finished savaging it,' said Oscar.

'Oh my Gosh. I am, aren't I!' She threw her head back, her long blonde hair falling behind her. With her free hand she covered her mouth and started shaking with laughter.

Oscar pretended to grab the doughnut from her, putting her in a comfortable headlock. Eva's head jerked back in a fit of laughter, their noses meeting.

'Stop!' she ripped her head loose. 'I win fights against my brother you know.'

'Is he asleep when you fight?' asked Oscar.

'She grabbed the doughnut back from him and shoved it back into the paper bag. She looked up to him and removed it delicately, presenting it to him once more.

'*One* bite.'

Oscar tilted his head forward and she raised the morsel to him, proudly. He took a bite and her nose scrunched.

'Pretty good.'

'The doughnut?' she asked, her lips apart.

'No. How you managed to get your arms all the way up here.'

Eva slapped his arm, leaving her hand on him for a moment.

'What ride are we going on?' she asked.

'Whatever you want. Unless you're in a rush to get back home to your boyfriend.'

Eva actioned marching off, and Oscar turned to walk home, following suit. She came back to him, tilting her head.

'Can I pick first?' she asked, her eyes flitting between the attractions. She darted two steps in one direction, and then three in another, before returning to Oscar.

'As long as it's not that fuck off thing!' she shouted, reaching into the evening air, pointing at the rusted tower. Her black cardigan fell momentarily to reveal her wrists, which she sharply propped back up.

Like a moth to a flame in the dwindling light, Eva ventured to the bumper cars. The screeching of which was cacophonous. Children lurched up into the air almost a foot above their seats as their father's hurtled into them, bounding from their kin to the steel wall which barred the arena.

Her expression became one of concern. She left the scene, and Oscar followed her closely, pulling her to his side to guide her through the swathes of people.

'The Waltzer! Have you been on this one?' asked Eva.

Lilies Of The Damned

'Maybe.'

'Maybe?'

'It's been a long time, I can't remember.' Oscar recalled the time he was violently sick after departing from the ride, some years back.

Eva's eyes widened.

'Fine,' said Oscar.

He went over to the man sat next to the spinning ride in a dainty glass compartment, showered in fibrils of shadows which danced between the lights. The man's eyes were fixated on the teacups that spun ceremoniously before him.

'How's it going. Could I get two tickets for this ride?' asked Oscar.

'Five,' the showman said.

'Five what, each?' asked Oscar.

'No, for two.'

Oscar retrieved his wallet, pulling it close to his chest as he counted the correct change.

'Here.'

The showman took the change.

'What do we do now? Just get on when they get off, I assume?'.

The showman nodded.

He returned to Eva. Shortly after, the dazzled partakers got up from their teacups as the ride slowed; deliriously making their way off. The pair picked their teacup quickly, pushing against one another as the safety bar was placed down on them by the showman.

'Put your phone in here,' Eva said hurriedly, motioning to her small black shoulder bag, tapping it with a long fingernail persistently.

'Na it's all good, It's —'.

Their teacup spun cyclically in rapid succession. Eva's head lurched forward and then back, arriving upon Oscar's shoulder, where it remained for the duration of the ride.

The black of night flashed as the heavens burned.

Oscar reached for Eva's fingertips prudently as they walked back to her house through town. She took up his hand meaningfully.

'I don't like holding hands, it cringes me out,' said Eva.
'Neither do I. But I thought it was the done thing.'
'Have you not done this a lot?'
'Well, it's only on once a year—'.
'You know what I mean,' said Eva.
Oscar's lips curled at either side, letting go of her hand.
'No, I'll do it,' spouted Eva, curling her fingers round his again.
Oscar willed his free arm to stop shaking as the couple turned the corner at the bottom of the hill, finding themselves on the home straight.
'Are you up early?' asked Oscar.
'Yeah, I've got to go into town; I have work.'
'Where do you work?'
'Shoe shop.'
'Any good?'
'It's okay. It's just money, isn't it?'
Oscar turned Eva's head to face his and gently pressed his lips against hers. She tasted of soap and cherries. Her mouth was cold, and he would have ended his life here if he were to ever be in control of such a decision. They embraced, and she kissed him back intently, only applying the same pressure as he.
'Shall I walk you to your door?' asked Oscar.
'No. You can stop at the bench,' said Eva.
'Do you want to stay at mine?' he asked.
'I do, but I haven't got my stuff for work.'
'I'll wait here for you.'
She checked the time on her golden watch, 'I'll be like twenty minutes though?'
'That's fine.'

By the time the young couple arrived at Oscar's house, a silver lunar light was upon them.
'Can I get you a drink?' asked Oscar.
'What have you got, juice?'
'Apple or orange.'

Lilies Of The Damned

'Apple please.'

'I don't have apple.'

'Orange then!'

Oscar went to the kitchen and scrubbed a glass clean, filling it with orange juice. He shouted in the direction of the hall: 'Head up to my room, if you want!'

To which he heard back. 'Can I use your bathroom?'

'Up the stairs, you can't miss it!'

Oscar arrived at his room with the glass in hand, kicking everything that was awry under his bed. He swiveled his monitor round to face his bed, and religiously checked his sheets and pillows for any marks, after which, leaving the glass on the side for Eva. He turned on his Xbox and hunted for a film boring enough to watch.

Eva entered the room as Oscar was thumbing a disc. She looked around cautiously and placed herself on the end of his bed.

'Your drink is there.'

She took the glass and pressed her nose to the rim, taking a careful sip, before returning to the end of the bed. Oscar slid the disc into His Xbox and grabbed the remote. He stood over the machine; it made familiar whirring sounds. To his relief, it loaded up and he hopped onto his bed, dumping himself between the pillows.

Eva was still perched far from him, like a stray.

'You can come up here if you want?'

She was silent.

'I don't bite,' he added.

'No, you just kiss unsuspecting girls,' said Eva.

Oscar pulled her closer and turned the sound up on the remote.

'Your Mum isn't back, is she?' asked Eva.

'No, she's away at the minute.'

'At the minute! As in, she's coming back tonight?'

'No, she's away for a while, I think,' said Oscar.

'How do you think, surely that's something you would know?'

Oscar nuzzled her fleshy cheek with his knuckle.

'You smell lovely.'

Lilies Of The Damned

'Thanks. I wasn't expecting to stop out.'
'Stop out?'
'It means stay over.'
'How have I never heard that before?'
'Everyone says stop out. How long have you lived in Kellwell?'
'Ages.'
'Your accent sounds further South though.'
Oscar blushed a pale pink. 'It is. I'm from Kent originally.'
'Yeah, I can still hear it, a bit.'
He fiddled with the remote, fiddling with the volume until it felt right.
'This looks boring Oscar.'
'It is. I had to study it.'
'Why would you put this on, then?'
She rolled atop his chest smiling, her large eyes penetrating any façade he might propose. Any dominion he had over her, melted, thawing in the outlandish gaze of her eyes.
'It's such a doddle though, isn't it. Studying English, or Film, or any of those subjects.' She said, exhaling on Oscar's neck.
'It is, but I failed them.'
'Oh yeah! You resat the year.'
Oscar placed his hands gently at either side of Eva's head, rubbing his thumbs into the crevices of her temples. He looked upon her, carefully.
'What are you doing?' asked Eva.
She eyed him playfully, turning her head to the side, resting it on him. Oscar leant towards her and kissed the top of her head, only prising his lips away from her forehead as she looked up at him.
He felt her curvaceous form wrap round him. They sat up together and kissed furiously.
'Wait,' said Eva.
'What?'
'Let me brush my teeth and get ready for bed.'
Oscar fell back, letting his head sink into the depths of his pillows as

Eva went into the bathroom. He nursed a painful erection that burrowed into his jeans.

She returned, dressed in a long black tee shirt with black embroidered pants.

He embarked upon her and addressed her body lasciviously.

He ran his hands beneath her embroidered cloth as she lay before him. She held the sleeves of her shirt down, arching her back, placing her legs upon his shoulders, her toes curled. It was not long before he entered her, she bit down on her bottom lip and the night sung. She murmured Oscar's name, and he was overcome by an orgastic intensity; one that could never be replaced.

He rolled to her side, and they embraced.

He decided he would die for her.

Eva's alarm sounded, awaking Oscar first. He watched her sleeping for a moment before she came to her senses.

Her eyes opened and she dashed into the bathroom without saying a word, returning in her ensemble for the day: a black jumper and leggings.

'You're so gorgeous it pains me,' said Oscar.

She smiled at him, pushing her hair behind one of her ears.

'Does that mean you're going to make me breakfast?'

Oscar dropped his hand to the side of the bed, searching for his boxer shorts.

'Don't push it.'

'Quickly though, I've got to get the bus from Hawthorne soon'.

Oscar got dressed and brushed his teeth. He hurried into the kitchen and started cooking bacon.

Eva waited in the living room initially, but he soon felt her breath on his neck and turned round to see her stood on her tiptoes looking over his shoulder.

'You're going to overcook it—flip it!'

'Am I doing it, or are you, Eva?' asked Oscar slowly.

'You're doing it, but I can do it better.'

Oscar rolled his eyes, relieving himself of a smirk.

When ready, he handed her the plated sandwich, to which she covered in ketchup, and plucked a knife and fork from the drawer, setting herself down at the dining room table; she cut into it, dismembering the bread within the entrails of the red sauce.

'Do you want any sandwich with that ketchup?' he asked.

She looked back over her shoulder at him, chuckling wildly.

'I love ketchup.'

he thought to say: I love you.

PART TWO - LOVE

CHAPTER FOUR

TO BE LOVED

It was a cold evening; Autumn had eaten the tail of Summer, and both Richard and Fred were sat within Oscar's living room.

Oscar's phone sounded.
'Did I leave my top at yours?'
'I don't think so.'
'Well, can you have a look for me now?'
'I can't right now, but I will in a sec.'
'Oscar, look now'.
'Shush.'
He hung up and went upstairs. He searched a pile of clothes strewn about his room, rooting through them diligently to no avail.
He rang Eva back.
'I have looked—I promise.'
'Oh Oscar! I wanted to wear that later!'
'Surely you have another one?'
'Not that one though! I fucking know it's there as well.'

'You have loads of the same top. It's not here, I promise.'

'Can you look properly please? I'll be so annoyed if I need to buy another one.'

'Eva, I can absolutely assure you, that your top is not here,' Oscar ran his eyes sparingly across his room. 'I have hardly any clothes anyway, it can't have gotten lost amongst them?'

'Maybe your Mum has it?'

'My Mum isn't stealing your clothes.'

Oscar slid his phone back into his pocket, walked over to his bedroom window and pressed his palms against the glass. Outside, the dew of the morn persisted. The skies were hoary, and the clouds ashen. He plucked his hands willfully from the glass, leaving behind watery marks that fell like tears.

'It's not too early for this, is it?' Fred asked to none other than himself, as he cracked a silver tin. The contents of the beer shot up and gushed over the pull tab.

'Mouth over it,' said Oscar.

Fred's lips were drowned under the froth as he wrestled with the can.

Richard was sitting, entrenched within a tan cushion. From which, he looked up at Oscar drearily.

'Everything alright with Eva?'

'Fine.'

'What did she want?'

'Just lost her top or something'.

'Is that your fault?' asked Richard.

Oscar shrugged and went to the kitchen, pulling a bottle of vodka from the freezer, alongside a cheap bottle of cola from the fridge before returning.

'Do you want any of this?' he asked, holding both bottles to the air.

'I thought it was left out; is it rank?' asked Richard.

'Freezer job,' confirmed Oscar.

Richard looked at his phone before meeting his eyes.

'I guess so.'

Oscar poured up two glasses of the liquor, topping them off with cola.

Richard spluttered as soon as the drink touched his tongue.

'Are you trying to kill me?'

'Not you,' said Oscar.

Fred took a swag of the drink, using the remainder of his beer as a chaser. 'That's how we like it! Isn't it?' he gulped from the glass like a parched fish. 'Who do you think will win the fight later? I might put a bet on.'

Oscar adjusted his black cap. 'I'm honestly not sure.'

'I don't know either. How much do you put on normally?' asked Richard.

'A lot. It depends, doesn't it?'

Oscar's phone rang again; he sloped out to the hallway.

'Y'ello.'

'I'm just going to buy another one. I know you've lost it.'

A pause commenced.

'Are you going to pay for it, then?' asked Eva.

'How much is it?'

'I can probably find one for thirtyish.'

'I paid for us to go to London the other week,' said Oscar.

'Not all of it?'

'Most,' Oscar flipped his cap round. 'Just get it, we'll sort it out later.'

'Okay, thanks, bye—'.

'Wait, what time are you grabbing your stuff from here?'

'In the next hour probably.'

'Okay, Fred and Richard are here, by the way'.

'Okay,' said Eva, resoundingly.

Two hours went by, before the knock on the door came.

Fred cocked his small eye and looked out the window.

'Have you got the brass here for me?'

'Pull your pants down a bit,' Oscar said, as he got to his feet.

He opened the door, and there Eva stood. She had fake eyelashes on, and her face was powdered a tanned bronze. Her nose was snatched, and her lips pursed.

'How are you doing Evie?' said Oscar.

'Don't call me Evie.'

A roar of laughter erupted from the living room.

He put his arm round her shoulders and guided her upstairs.

'How was work?' he asked.

'Have you been drinking?'

'We have, aye.'

'Yeah, it was okay.'

'It beats cleaning out bins though?' Oscar smirked.

'Yeah! But you only do that twice a week. And it's like a few hours at a time.'

'If I didn't, who would pay for all the tops you lose?'

'Oscar, please. You're always fucking losing stuff.'

Upon entering his room, he ripped out thirty pounds from his wallet, dropping it on his bed before her.

'What time are you back later?' he asked.

'I don't know, it's Layla's birthday'.

'Layla?'

'*Ha*-ha,' replied Eva.

'What time though? In all seriousness,' Oscar turned his head away from her. 'It's not the end of the world, if it's late. I think the fight starts at two.'

'I should be back before then.'

He turned to face her again. Looking upon her powdered mien, intently.

'You look so good.'

She hopped onto the bed and gave him a smacking kiss on the lips. He gripped her and went to her neck.

'I can't. I've got all my makeup on.'

'Is that not for me?'

'Nope,' she said, smiling, her eyelids relaxing and her cheeks curling.

'You're stewing'.

'I'm not stewing,' Oscar said, as he pushed at his eyebrows with his middle finger and his thumb. 'I'll have you later, anyway'.

She hugged him and he picked her up and placed her on the floor fondly.

'I love you,' said Oscar.

'I love you too,' said Eva, prodding her index finger painfully at his heart. 'Do you remember the first time you said that to me?'

'Your version of events is different to mine,' replied Oscar.

'No! you were going, *love you, love you, love you, love you, I love you, love you,*' She continued, keeping her finger pressed against his chest. 'It slipped out! And we were eating a Chinese at the time.'

'The only bit I remember, is you telling me that I ate like a fucking pig,' said Oscar.

'You do eat like a fucking pig.'

'You should stick your head in downstairs and say hello before you leave.'

'They should say hello to me.'

'Can you just do it, please.'

'Fine,' Eva said, sighing.

The couple descended the stairs and Eva put her hand against the frame of the living room door, peering across the room.

'Eva! There she is,' said Fred.

Oscar gripped the handle of the door until his knuckles turned a hot white.

'You okay Eva?' asked Richard.

'Yes, I'm fine thank you. Are you?' before Richard could reply, Fred interjected.

'Oh, you know me, keeping on, keeping on. It's the same story.'

Eva smiled warmly, looking back at Oscar.

'I've got to go anyway. It was nice seeing you both.'

Oscar shut the door behind his friends and kissed the top of her head.

'I'll walk you back.'

'No, you don't need to.'
'I want to, though'.
'No, honestly—'.
'Shut up,' said Oscar.

Oscar returned and stood outside his front door, his hands scrambling within his wallet for his key. He could hear the booming voice of Fred, but not Richard. It always surprised him how little sound windows blocked out. He reconsidered almost immediately; they're only made of glass after all.

He made his way to the living room and was met by a familiar sight.

'It will just be one for-a-hunna,' Fred said to his phone. His bulky frame was sliding off the sofa; his back lay almost completely flat across it. His legs were squatting on the floor beneath him and the weight of his body teetered precariously on the cushion ledge.

'Yes mate—Just one for a hunna. But you're about all day aren't you? So, make sure to keep your phone on!'

Fred's joyous laughter almost dismantled him from his position.

'You know what they say mate; you know what they say about me.'

'That you're washed up,' said Oscar.

Fred did not afford him a look.

'As soon as possible! How long will you be?'

Oscar interrupted. 'Bro. Do not give him my address. Go pick it up at the corner shop down the road.'

'Can you drop off at the corner shop. Near Hawthorne Gardens?' asked Fred.

Fred hung up and clambered back up the sofa, his stomach spilling out from the bottom of his tee.

'Yep, no issues. He's a sound guy in fairness to him. What would we do without Danny Cross?'

What would we do without Danny Cross? Oscar mused to himself.

Fred pulled out an icy bag from his back pocket. He waved it in the air until the bright flakes within became unstuck from the plastic, rejoining the snowy mass at the bottom of the bag. He pinched it securely and flicked it with his other hand.

'Do you want some?' asked Fred.

'I do,' said Oscar. 'But I shouldn't. Maybe later, if you get some more.'

'Suit thyself,' replied Fred.

A moment passed, unbound from the march of time.

'Richard, can you drive to the shop, he'll be there soon?' asked Fred, sparingly.

Oscar pointed to Richard. His friend was now sat with both arms hanging from the sofa, as though they were too heavy for him to raise.

'This Richard?' Oscar asked.

'Yes,' Fred confirmed.

Oscar moved closer to Richard, and lifted one of his friend's limp arms up, showing it to Fred as if it were testament enough.

'He can't drive, can he? We'll walk.'

Richard gargled hyperbolically: 'No, I can drive.'

'Not worth it. We'll walk,' demanded Oscar.

With this, he ushered his friends out into the grim light of day, before immediately retreating to grab a coat.

'Keem on,' Fred said, as he languished on the driveway.

The trio set off.

'He's really well connected, Dan Cross, you know?'

'I did not,' Oscar said, hoping this would spell the end of Fred's infatuation with Dan Cross.

'He's got links with people in the city. He's not just a runner, he can get anything.'

'Can he pick me up some bog roll,' said Oscar.

'Mate, honestly, he's a sound guy as well. He's seriously connected.'

Fred blathered incongruously to a swaying Richard as Oscar dropped back to check his phone.

He had received a message from Eva; stating that she had 'massively fucked up.' His fingers tapped against his phone screen rapidly, holding it in a vice-like grip as he stared at the screen ominously.

Lilies Of The Damned

Fred turned to face him, stretching his tee shirt down over his burgeoning midriff.

'She's probably just in the blender mate.'

Oscar put his phone away and lifted his cap to the sky to ruffle his hair. Richard approached and rested his arm on his shoulder.

'All good?'

'Course,' said Oscar.

Parked outside the shop was a battered silver car. Oscar recognised the vehicle from many moons ago and tapped pointedly in its direction.

'I know that car; it's what's his chops.'

'Mutton chops,' answered Richard.

'No! It's that Red guy's car.' Oscar confirmed.

'Surely he's not out already?' Richard asked, bobbing to his knees to check the registration number, almost falling to the gravel.

'It's his car, he lives close to Eva. But I've not seen it parked there, in, what—three months, maybe more?'

'He might've been caught and he's on bail now?' Richard asked, bemused, as though he had lost the words he had spoken and wanted them returned immediately.

'It's been some months now, hasn't it? All we do is repeatedly say he's on bail each time the conversation comes up,' Oscar zipped his coat up and down incessantly. 'He must have been caught, because like I say, he wasn't at his house for months.'

He walked over to Richard, yanking him up to his feet. 'Careful, he's probably inside the shop?'

Fred looked up from his phone. 'Dan Cross will be here in a minute.'

Oscar looked at Fred. 'Why do you keep calling him Dan Cross, why not just call him Dan?'

'Because it's Dan Cross,' answered Fred, who now walked to the side of the silver car, inspecting it. 'It's like the NeverEnding Story with this cunt.'

'Come on, we're best off going inside. We don't want to look strange stood about his car,' concluded Oscar.

The boys entered the shop and separated. Richard hung about the door, and Fred went to the fridges at the back, whilst Oscar walked down the nearest aisle.

Oscar kept on the lookout for Red, but lost interest in the matter as soon as he checked his phone; Eva was yet to reply to him. He gritted his teeth and prepped another message. Asking her if she was okay, with an additional row of question marks.

His path was blocked.

'Alright?'

'I'm good,' said Oscar, looking up at the gruff man, whose voice was deep, like his.

'Good day for it, isn't it?' inquired Red politely.

Oscar performed a smile with one side of his face.

'It always is.'

Red stood to the side and Oscar walked on by, arriving at the end of the shop. He waited for the sound of the shop bell and car to start up outside, before turning round.

He returned to the door and nodded in acknowledgement to Richard who was now leaning against a rack of magazines. They shared a portentous look with one another.

'Where's Fred?' asked Oscar.

'Where do you think?' Retorted Richard.

'You go sort him out, I need to ring someone,' Oscar exited the shop. The air smelt of petrol, and a line of oil now bled out onto the road, curling left.

He rang Eva and waited...no reply. He tried again but was met once more by a persistent ringing.

'Fuck me,' Oscar whispered to himself and conjured another text, this time, addressing her behaviour.

The three met outside and Fred dumped a selection of bottles onto Richard. Fred then looked to the sky and spoke: 'he's here.'

'I left the red carpet at home; I'll not be long,' said Oscar.

Fred's thick fingers rummaged about his wallet, pulling out multiple sheets of tender. 'Our lord and savior will not be mocked.'

He looked to Oscar's feet.

'Can one of you come with me? Dan can drop us back after.'

'He won't drop us back, but I'll come with,' said Oscar, giving his house key to Richard. 'If anything happens to me, tell everyone I know, they were just the worst.'

'You won't be long, will you? How long does this normally take?' asked Richard, who spoke in a manner which echoed grave concern.

'I couldn't tell you,' said Oscar.

He joined Fred and they departed from Richard's sight.

'It was Red in the shop,' said Oscar.

'Yeah, I know, I spoke to him. He's alright in fairness,' replied Fred.

'He's just not though, is he.' Oscar retorted.

'There he is, look!' Fred pointed ahead at a white Subaru parked at the back of the shop. Oscar zipped his jacket to its brim and pulled his cap down to the point it now sat above his hooded eyelids, covering his brow. He dumped his hands into his pockets, taking flank beside his friend.

Fred approached the car window with a strident laugh: 'Danny boy!'

'Rate,' the driver said, as he peered out the gap of his window. There was hardly enough room for one to push their fingers through, but somehow his bulbous eyes almost crawled out their sockets and fell through the opening.

'Busy day is it?' asked Fred.

'I'm not your taxi driver, am I?' the driver retorted, winding down more of his window; revealing his patchy stubble and long jaw.

Fred laughed cheerfully, placing his hand atop the vehicle, leaning in closer to Danny's face. Oscar saw the suspension dip and took a step back.

'Get your hand off it,' said Danny.

'Sorry mate. I'll get you another if I break it.'

Oscar shot Danny a glance, who unlocked the doors. Fred pulled open the front passenger door and entered. Oscar prowled to the back door and opened it, scanning the seats for any needles that might end up in his rear.

Danny revved the engine disdainfully as Oscar scurried for his seat belt; managing to fasten it before the car bolted out of the car park across the junction.

'Where are you wanting to go?' asked Fred.

'Skate Park,' said Danny.

Fred only waited a moment more before speaking: 'What you on with today anyway?'

Though he may as well have asked the glove box. The silence was painful. The only aid to which, was the occasional clunking of Fred's back against his seat each time Danny applied the brakes sparingly.

They arrived at Kellwell's skate park and Danny pulled in behind a set of trees, obscuring the view one might have if they were to look at the car from the adjoining leisure centre.

'What do you want then?' asked Danny.

'I think I might have to get more than I planned for. It's always a longer day than you think, innit?'

The car smelt of peaches, and Oscar sighted a peach emoji air freshener hanging from the rearview mirror confirming his suspicion. He was suitably impressed with his olfaction, but remained dejected that he would not be able to escape from the car; the doors were now locked. However, he was certain he would be able to choke out Danny from behind. Or, at the very least, hold him still whilst Fred wailed on him. This was under the assumption Danny was not armed.

Danny reached over and clicked the glove box; it dropped open in front of Fred, revealing a set of bags and other paraphernalia.

'I thought you might want more,' said Danny; his laugh sounded like a tire puncture.

'You know me too well,' Fred said, handing him the appropriate cash, taking the bags. 'We're just up the hill —'.

Oscar piped up: 'We're good, thanks. We'll walk from here.'

The pair exited the car and slammed the doors behind them. They walked to a side alley, and Fred pulled out one of the bags.

'Look at the size of that bastard.'

Fred inspected the white gold, before placing it firmly back into the depths of his wallet.

'You're fucking joking me,' Oscar said, looking at his phone.

'I'm not. It's honking.'

Fred fingered his wallet again.

Oscar threw him an eye. 'Not that.'

He had a missed call from Eva, but when he tried to call her back, he was met once more with no answer.

'Fuck my wank existence,' said Oscar.

'It's shit innit,' Fred agreed.

'Everything is.'

They arrived back at the house to find Richard stood over the sink guzzling from a glass of water.

Oscar grabbed the victim's waist, pretending to penetrate him.

'Melt.'

'It's looking slow,' Richard confirmed.

'It's not for this guy,' Oscar said, nodding his head back at Fred, who was currently lining his goods across the dining room table. 'What goes up and never comes down?'

'Fred,' said Richard.

Oscar approached the table, standing at the fiend's side. The three of them looked on at the white splendor of contents which were drawn like snowy hills across the wood under an olive-coloured vase, filled with his mother's white lilies.

Oscar flipped his cap back to front and put his hands loosely upon his waist; his splayed fingers resting on the trimmings of his black pockets. He bent his knees slightly and addressed the others.

'Yeah. I'm having some of this.'

'You actually?' Richard asked, with an expression of amusement and perplexion.

'I am. I'm suicidal.'

'He is,' Fred said.

'I might also.' said Richard.

Lilies Of The Damned

Fred looked to each of them, his clunky head turning at first to Richard and then to Oscar, his cheeks flapping at the velocity in which he turned.

'Well, I'm glad you lot are having some of my stuff I just bought.'

'We'll obviously give you some cash for it, won't we?' Oscar looked to Richard for confirmation, who stood in a daze.

'Definitely,' Richard said, finally.

'Should I get a gret' big *muggins* tattoo on my head?' asked Fred.

They laughed in unison.

'You know I love you both; Uncle loves you both. Of course you can have some. You'll be done off a couple anyway. This is rocket fuel; this is real Columbian rocket fuel.'

Oscar turned his hat back round, so that the brim now cast shade on his face: 'Right,' he said, unassured.

'Barn door, please?' asked Fred.

Oscar pulled the artifact of much repute from his wallet and handed it to Fred. With the key now in the fiend's possession, he plucked a bag from the table and passed it to Richard.

'Dinner is served.'

The eve darkened and frost covered the empty driveway. Many cans and bottles now littered the living room floor.

Fred leant over a seated Oscar, managing to position his head out of the window before lighting a cigarette; a gust of cold air shooting in through it. The trio's beer jacket's shielding them from the chill.

Oscar was nursing his palpitations on the sofa, checking his phone intermittently.

'Is any totty coming later?' asked Fred, his trousers falling to his ankles.

He pulled them back up in haste, so he could return to his cigarette.

'I think Eva might bring a couple of mates back, I'm not sure.'

Fred's attention turned to Richard, who was sat on the floor resting his back against the radiator.

'Could you be any more boring Richard?'

'I wouldn't test him,' said Oscar.

Richard stood up. 'I'm actually feeling sober after that gear'.

'It's a bit of a dance,' Fred said. 'You have to drink when you feel a bit too sharp and take more when you feel a wobble coming on.'

Oscar felt a vibration within his pocket and legged it upstairs.

'Eva?'

'Hey, can you hear me?'

He glanced at the time. 'I can, but you're really muffled.'

There was further distortion before Eva replied.

'Oscar, I'm so fucked up'.

'I can tell—what's been happening? Why haven't you replied to me?'

'I'm so fucked you know.'

Oscar breathed deeply. 'Have you taken anything?'

'I don't even know; I think I've been spiked.'

'How do you not know if you've taken anything? What do you mean you've been spiked?'

'I'm so fucked, I'm eating some chips to sober up.'

He remained quiet.

'This guy fully put himself on me.'

His face turned white.

'How?'

'I didn't do anything.'

'What do you mean by that?'.

'I can't speak about this right now, you sound so angry.'

'I'm not exactly over the fucking moon, am I? Stop changing the subject—what do you mean he put himself on you?'

'These guys just came over and started talking to us: Layla and I, we were trapped in the booth.'

'Go on,' Oscar said, with his eyes shut.

'I was talking to one of them, I was just being polite, and he caught me completely off guard.'

'Caught you off guard how?'

'I was trapped in the booth, and he leant over and kissed me.'

Lilies Of The Damned

Oscar placed his head against the cool wall of his bedroom, squinting his eyes shut as tightly as he could.

'But Oscar, I didn't kiss him back. I was so disgusted when he did it.'

He breathed in carefully and exhaled deeply.

'Okay.'

'Honestly, it's just made me realise again how much I love you. Do you love me?'

'Yes.'

'I just want to be with you now, I don't even want to be out! I'll see if we can get back any earlier.'

He remained quiet.

'Thing is, it's Layla's birthday, I can't exactly leave her. Are we both still okay to go to yours later?'

'Fine.'

'Okay, love you,' said Eva.

He dropped his phone to the floor and squashed his cheek against the wall, a tear welling in his eye. He clawed at his face and felt his lower half enfeeble. He felt the running of his blood under his skin and could not tell if he was hot or cold.

He retrieved his phone. He had received a message from Eva, declaring her love for him. He sat as still as a gargoyle at the end of his bed. A strange relief now overcame him; was this the worst pain he could bear? Could there be, a worse pain, and could he bear it? There could be, he thought. But surely none he would have to contend with. Eva loved him of course, he believed she did, truly.

He stood up and punched the wall. He was convinced one of his knuckles had moved, but the agony diminished to a dull ache shortly after he sat back down.

'What are you doing up here?' The call came from Richard, who had marched up the stairs, taking a seat on the bed next to him.

'Catching my breath.'

'My heart is going at a hundred miles an hour,' said Richard.

'Mine was earlier. Now it's stopped.'

'Completely?'

'Yeah.'

'Fred told me I should drink through it. I think I might have to.'

Oscar stretched his legs out in front of him and looked at his socks. He wiggled a big toe that protruded through a hole in the cotton.

'What time is Eva coming back?' asked Richard.

'Not sure,' said Oscar, putting his hands upon his thighs. 'How do you feel when Fran is out?'

'I just distract myself.'

'Do you ever get jealous?'

'Not really anymore.'

'Must be nice.'

'She doesn't go out a lot.'

Oscar received a text from Eva, notifying him she was nearing the house. The time was now one o' clock in the morning. Fred was sluggishly scooping out what remained from a bag, and Richard was trying to find the right channel for the fight.

Oscar heard murmuring outside the house and opened the front door to reveal Eva and her friend. Their hands were clasped round their arms, shaking.

He ushered them inside and Eva brushed off a meagre amount of snow that rested on her bare shoulders.

'We were waiting ages!' she exclaimed.

Layla afforded Oscar a smile, 'hi Oscar.'

'Hey Layla. How was your night?'

'It was good! Eva was fucked though.'

He looked at Eva, who looked back at him. They held each other's gaze for a moment before he broke away from her stare.

'Do you want me to put anything upstairs for you both?' Oscar asked.

'We'll do it in a minute,' Eva said, her dilated pupils crossing the glass of her eyes.

'Do you want some juice, or something, or a drink?' Oscar asked again, in the pair's general direction.

'I don't know if I should drink anymore,' said Eva, still shuddering melodramatically. 'Are you having something Layla?'

'Yeah, I'll have a glass of wine if you are.'

'I think there's some about. I'll check.' Oscar declared.

He departed to the kitchen, while Eva and her friend went upstairs. He found a bottle of wine and poured out two glasses. He leant over the kitchen sink with one hand and with his other, pushed his palm into his nose forcefully. The strength in his legs was fading and he pulled at his hair that hung over his brow.

Eva entered behind him; she was now adorned in a cerulean dressing gown wrapped tightly round her midriff. She cocked her head to the side and looked at him, her expression akin to that of a manikin, her features in perfect harmony. He stood over her, handing her the glass of wine, making sure it was fitted within her grasp before letting go. He dropped his forehead slowly to hers and whispered to her.

'I'm not good.'

She held his look, her head pressed against his; sipping from the glass. She smelt like the Autumn rain.

'You know I would have stopped it if I could have.'

Oscar balanced his chin on her head, looking up at the ceiling. A tear welled in his eye once more. He did not allow himself to say what he wanted to.

'I feel like it's tainted.'

She pulled her head out from under his, turning away.

'How can you say that?' she asked, sharply.

'It's just how I feel.' Oscar said, with a look of betrayal.

She returned to him, attempting to grasp the back of his neck with her free hand. He moved his head to the side, and she kissed his cheek. Her damp lips imprinting a red shape on his face.

'It's making me weak,' he pleaded.

'I don't know what to say Oscar, I'm going upstairs with Layla. Let me know when that fight starts, I'll watch it if I'm up.'

She took the second glass and departed, leaving him alone in the kitchen. He could hear the ticking of the clock above him, the hum of the light behind him and the infrequent chatter of his friends in the living room. He grabbed a kitchen towel and bit down on it as hard as he could, to the point he could feel his canines becoming displaced.

His breathing quickened and he hoisted himself onto the kitchen table. He considered texting Richard to join him but resisted.

'I'm not well.'

He repeated to himself.

'I'm not.'

He rocked back and forth, tensing his calves. He Reached inside the cupboard for a glass and started to fill it with tap water, but dashed it across the sink, opting instead to drink a half empty can of lager.

Upon return to the living room, Fred was looking dangerous, teetering on the edge of the sofa.

'Are they here?'

Fred's dimwitted expression concealed little.

'Have you found the channel yet Rich?' asked Oscar.

'I have, it's just the prelims at the minute. It's starting soon though.'

Oscar set himself down next to Richard, and heard the pattering of feet on the staircase, which proceeded to the dining room.

'Going for a slash,' Fred said, rising to his feet and leaving the room.

Oscar let his head flop behind him and stretched his arms across the back of the sofa. Richard started talking about something he vaguely cared about, but not enough to engage with meaningfully. He slapped himself across the face and turned to his friend who was still talking incessantly in his direction.

'I'm struggling.'

Richard's babbling ceased. 'Yeah, I don't feel great.'

'I would put my life savings on you, not feeling as bad as me,' Oscar said, getting to his feet.

He overheard a conversation in the dining room and approached in a circumspect fashion. He leant his head against the doorframe to witness Fred with his arm across the table, looking at Eva lecherously, who stood silently with two empty glasses of wine in hand.

'How did he manage to get you?' Fred asked her sluggishly.

Oscar entered the room unseen, Fred's only course of action still, to leer at Eva.

It became too much for him to bear; he lunged forward spearing Fred in the base of his spine, who staggered forward in shock, the weight of Oscar thrusting him through the air. The pair crashed forth, narrowly missing Eva, colliding against the table. They clawed and spiraled with each other; their forms toppling against one another in every direction like a spinning coin. Fred fell, his babyish head hitting the edge of the table as he went to ground. Oscar jumped on top of him, mantling his reeling body and digging his knees fiercely into the fringes of his gut.

Eva's shrill scream sounded, and he hesitated, to which Fred retorted by throwing a weighty punch at his jaw. He bowed his head, and the punch narrowly missed his chin, instead deflecting across his cheekbone and drawing blood.

He nestled his head into Fred's chest, smearing blood across his friend's top. He pressed his torso against the floundering mass, and spurred by his bloodlust, beat him relentlessly, slugging unflinchingly at his friend's face. They exchanged barrages, and blood sprayed from Oscar's lips, coating Fred's aghast lemony eyes.

He felt the comforting grip of Richard's hands under his armpits, dragging him from Fred's body.

All he could hear was a distant ringing, all he could see was Eva's heart shaped face screaming at him, and all he could feel was the familiar touch of her hands, his back against the wall.

PART TWO - LOVE

CHAPTER FIVE

ADORED

Oscar awoke next to Eva in his bed. Layla was sleeping on the mattress against the wall, and he assumed Richard was in the other room. One side of his face ached, and he struggled to close his right hand. His mouth was dry and so was the well of his thoughts.

He reached over to Eva's golden locks which lay sprawled beside him. She lay still and he clawed himself closer to her beating body that resisted him. He locked his arm round her front, running a finger down her arm, to which he received a push from her foot. But still he held her, longingly.

Richard and Layla left shortly after waking. Little was said by the pair. Oscar asked Eva to stay with him longer; she obliged, reluctantly.

The couple lay in his bed, looking vacantly at the ceiling above. The chilling light of day shone over them, and they shared an occasional cold embrace, which did little to give them warmth.

Eva spoke first.

'I want to cry; I feel so anxious.'

'Cry then.'

'Don't speak to me like that, please.'

'My words are the least of your concern. It's a good job I use my mouth for this, and not for kissing strangers.'

Eva was silent.

Oscar remained fixated on the ceiling, which he now noticed had accrued a significant number of cobwebs.

'I thought you got spiked. What happened to that?'

'Please, Oscar, I'm going to have a panic attack. Honestly.'

'You're ruining me,' said Oscar, his eyes filling with tears. He let them fall freely from his canthus so that they spilled over his cheek onto the mattress.

'You're ruining me!' Eva retorted.

'Are you insane?' asked Oscar, confident he already had his answer.

Eva breathed heavily and rolled off the bed to the floor, taking up a fetal position.

'I can't do this right now,' she wailed.

Oscar stood over her, 'what makes you think I can?'

'Let's just end it then, it's done.' Eva said, looking over her shoulder at him whilst rocking on her knees; her hands stuck somewhere beneath her.

Oscar's expression dropped from one of sternness to grief. 'Why would you say something like that?'

'Well, it's ruined, isn't it?' said Eva, flatly.

'But you…did it?'

'So I'll end it.'

'But you love me?' Oscar's voice cracked. He wiped at his tears furiously.

'Wait, just come back on the bed,' he pleaded, his bottom lip shaking. He took up position next to Eva and tried to unravel her from her makeshift ball.

'I don't want to. I think this will be for the best,' she rocked, teetering back and forth, to him, and then away from him.

'It won't be, just come up here, please,' he tried to lift her from the floor, but she resisted and panted heavily, to the point he could hear her lungs wheezing.

'Eva?'

'We can't do this anymore, I'm sorry.'

'What do you mean?' Oscar looked at her aimlessly. 'It was fine yesterday?'

'You're a psycho,' she started crying and whimpering incessantly. 'I don't even like you that much, you don't make me feel good.'

'But you said you loved me. You said you loved me yesterday?'

'Sometimes when we fuck, I fake it, and I think of other people.'

Oscar's tears poured from his round cheeks. He walked to the far wall and beat his palm against it until he was depleted. He let himself fall, succumbing to the mattress beneath him. He wrapped his head inside the quilt and screamed. He emerged after a minute, his face red and his lip quivering.

'Why would you ever say something like that to me?'

She stood up, shaking. 'I just don't feel it.'

Oscar looked at her confused and ashamed in equal parts.

'I bumped into someone I used to have a thing with from school the other day in Kellwell. We had a spark.'

'A spark?' Oscar inquired desperately, his red face burgeoning from his cocoon.

'It was just exciting, we had chemistry,' said Eva.

Oscar looked across his room confused, drawing the sheets as close as they would come to him. He hoped by swaddling himself, it would restrain him from ripping her face off.

'I have really bad thoughts,' said Eva.

'Why would you say all of these horrible things to me, and then say that?' asked Oscar desperately. He dried his tears on the sheets and stood. He ogled at the subject of his torment, feeling as though he had just wrestled with a legion of hell.

'I'm going to be sick,' said Eva. She scampered to the bathroom and locked the door behind her.

He followed her trail and slumped himself against the door, resting his kidney against the wood in a crumpled heap on the floor. He heard retching from within and the splattering of sick hitting the toilet bowl. What ensued, was muffled noises of heaving and gagging.

'Let me in, I'll help you,' Oscar banged on the door droopily; his desperate banging sounding more like tapping.

Silence persisted.

Oscar remained outside the bathroom door, balancing his phone on his knee.

'You're concerning me, I'm going to have to ring your parents,' he said, slowly.

'Don't you dare ring my fucking parents.'

'So, you can speak?' asked Oscar.

Eva cried and her crying was mournful to hear. He was saddened by her sounds.

She spluttered and wailed; he could hear her grip the toilet seat. Her cries so intense she lost her breath and gasped for air.

He held his head in his hands. 'What do you want me to do?' he asked.

'Leave me alone,' said Eva.

'You're in my house.' Oscar croaked.

Silence fell momentarily.

He could hear sounds which resembled that of scratching and shuffling.

'What are you doing?' he asked. But in truth, he did not care for her answer, regardless of what she was doing, she sat no more than a foot away from him behind the door. He sat still and waited, lulling between a state of drowsiness and restless slumber.

The door unlocked and he jumped to his feet; he twisted the door handle and pushed against it. It was jammed by something, but there was enough give for him to forcefully open it. He heaved against the wood, revealing, at the foot of the door a cluster of towels entrapping it.

The door swung open, and Eva was seated before him, her knees facing inwards and her feet facing outwards. She did not meet his eye and looked past him dreamily. A red puddle pooled under her, and her face was a phantom white. Her giant eyes cradled her small black pupils that swam in her Turquentine iris. Her lips were silvered, and her brow, lax.

Oscar knelt before her, landing on his kneecaps in front of the puddle of blood.

'Why are you doing this, Eva, lovely?'

She looked at him, her eyes glazing over.

She muttered to herself. 'If you ring anyone, I'll kill myself.'

Oscar clutched her wounded wrist, raising it to his eye. It was congealed and dark, and his mother's razor rested in the blood beneath them. He pressed down on her gash gently and arced his head down, placing his lips against his knuckles, clasping her arm tightly.

'It's not deep. It's fine now,' said Eva.

Oscar cradled her in his arms, looking at her white scarred flesh.

He hugged her remorsefully and kissed her salty lips. He deprived his heart, for his eyes were his God.

PART TWO - LOVE

CHAPTER SIX

TO FEEL

He did not pine for the passing of the relationship nor grieve Eva, respecting her wishes as gospel. For many days and nights, he reveled in the pain of an addict, tossing in a cold sweat upon his bed, awoken by dreams of shattered shores, and nightmares of bountiful pleasures.

On such days, the twilight tales unraveled like a tapestry before him. He relived these dreams in his waking hours, feeling the tips of the nightly daggers against his spine. A most delicate pain came from the dreams that saw him live out an eternity with Eva, under the shade of an oak. The roots of the great oak twisted around them, creating a perfect indenture for their young bodies; surrounded by a garth of white lilies and the childhood scent of a windy summer. And upon these nights of limbo, they made love and held hands, taken in by the ecstasy of forever.

He knew the only cure for this unbearable anguish was her. For she was the only respite he might find in his waking life.

The days passed ceaselessly, and when the nights came, there was naught to be done for his ailing mind. Reality melded into one linear strip of time, punctuated by the hallmarks of routine. The only constant was his desperate melancholy, for there was none to replace her. None shared her genetic code, wild temperament, or ruinous innocence of the damned.

It was on a rainy Tuesday that Oscar received a text from Eva. She told him plainly that she missed him and that she had made a mistake.

He was not overcome by relief but grieved for his manumit of pain. He looked at the screen of his phone; captivated by the dominion one could have over his life.

He paced across his room, reliving the moments of lust and misgivings which hung here. He knew he could love none after with the intensity he loved her. He knew, if this river was to run dry, then there he would lay, sullied within the drowned bed, for that is where he wished to be and all he was deserving of.

There was nowhere for him to retreat to, and no one to heed his words, for his thoughts were devised in a wicked web of machinations, and if a single silver thread were to be severed, all would fall.

He knew he would return to her, and he knew he would do so in earnest. With his doting on display, worn like a shield with many arrows embedded within. There was no quarrel that could penetrate his shield, and no weapon that could break it.

The grey light of the sun parted the clouds and a shower of rain fell to earth. He looked out to the unkempt lawn where a punctured football remained. He wondered how many cultures of insects and alike had been fostered under the ball, and how many had since been washed away. To imagine that there is something, and others, that exist apart from oneself is frightening. How could the machine of the universe bear all this information at once?

He dwelled in his melancholy, no stranger to the halls of the dejected. He immersed himself in these dying moments before replying to Eva.

He asked her if she wanted to see him. To which she replied: she did. She told him he could stay the night; her parents were away.

He agreed to these terms.

He readied an overnight bag and sat lonesomely on his bed until the early hours of the evening.

He walked through Kellwell, and made it to the bench, sighting Red's parked car before taking a right up Eva's road.

The evening air was brisk after the downpour, and Eva's bedroom window was open; open so wide that it looked as though one could climb up to it and enter.

He knocked on the door and waited patiently for her to answer. She quickly opened the door and he emerged into her home, soaked. He prised off his damp jumper, careful to not knock off his cap, and dropped it in a bundle on the floor next to his bag.

Her eyes were red and weary, her hair tied back and her make-up dark. She wore black leggings and a dark tee shirt. She folded her arms loosely and leaned against the wall to her left. Her face emanated warmth and her eyes lulled him closer.

'Are you cold?' she asked.

Before he could reply, she picked up the bundle of his belongings and carried them upstairs.

'I'm okay,' he said to the back of her escaping head.

He followed her up to her bedroom. It was spotlessly clean, to the point he felt guilty for dropping his wet bag on the floor downstairs. She placed his possessions in her wardrobe and tapped on the large glass aquarium next to the television. He saw her lizard resting within; he watched it spring from its docile state to bite the head of a motionless cricket.

'What have you been doing with yourself? Have you been seeing anyone?' asked Eva.

'No, I thought you needed this? I wanted you to have space.' Oscar's voice was hoarse, and he pulled his damp cap over his eyes.

'Of course,' said Eva, as she fussed with the handle of her wardrobe. 'I would never do that to you. Do you want to hug it out?'

Her lips curled and she jumped on his back, pulling him to the bed. She climbed on top of him; her legs sprawled across his and she nestled her head in the indent of his chest.

'I just don't know how it got to this,' Oscar said peacefully, placing his hand on her forehead as though he were checking her temperature.

'I'm just not in a good place, but I still love you,' Eva said.

Oscar bit down on his lip, managing to weather the storm of his wrath.

'I just wish you would show it.'

'I am! Now.'

She plucked his hand from the bed and kissed his fingers laboriously.

'I need to know this isn't going to happen again,' said Oscar.

'What isn't?'

'You know what. You can't do this to me, I can't live like this.'

She pressed her index finger against his lips, and he bit her hand playfully before casting it out of his mouth.

'I was thinking about drinking bleach.'

'You wouldn't have done that,' said Eva.

'Probably not, but I've lost friends over this.'

'He was never your friend anyway. A friend wouldn't talk down on you like that.'

'True. But am I not allowed to feel this way?'

Eva looked to her window, out across the darkening skies.

She pressed her deft ear against his chest. 'I can hear your heartbeat, Oscar.'

'Is it quick or slow?'

'Quite quick I think.'

'There's no way you can tell.'

'I can! But it's very faint'.

'Don't tell me about it, I'll pass out,' said Oscar.

She cackled. 'You're so squeamish!'

'I used to feint in year eight Science lessons, did I tell you?'

'Ages ago. That's so embarrassing though.'

They lay still and Oscar nursed her cheek with his knuckle.

'They used to have to remove me from class.'

'What makes you feel like you're going to feint?' asked Eva.

'The making babies part and the talk of red blood cells. All that jazz.'

'What do you think our baby is going to be like?'

Oscar sat up marginally, pulling Eva closer to him. She flopped back onto him like a ragdoll, and he thought about her question earnestly before replying.

'It's going to be absolutely fucked.'

Eva laughed hysterically.

'It's going to be ginger and insane,' she pulled her hair apart revealing her auburn roots.

'They're coming through a bit now, look.'

Oscar eased his being, exhaling deeply.

'Do you want a drink or something?' asked Eva.

'Have you got a beer?'

'One of my Dad's.'

'Yes please.'

Eva hopped from her perch, enabling him to stretch out his legs. He shook them out vehemently, fighting back the tingling sensation of paresthesia developing in his foot. She left the room, and he took the opportunity to inspect her Gecko up close. He pushed his nose close to the glass box and could feel the warmth of the heat lamps from the inside. In the corner of the cage, behind a large pebble was the Gecko's previous skin, the shedded husk had maintained its prior form and appeared alien.

Oscar scanned the surrounding interior, sighting the Gecko under a pebble, it still had the cricket's head in its mouth. The hind legs of the insect were writhing monotonously, as if it were only resisting its demise as a performance dedicated to him. The lizard moved the Cricket's thorax around its mouth; its lower jaw hoisting it further within, until the hindlegs of the insect disappeared.

Eva returned and handed him a beer. 'I forgot to get the bottle opener—'.

Oscar cracked the lid on the back of his teeth, removing it and putting it in his pocket.

'You're going to break your teeth doing that.'

'I've been told that for years,' Oscar said, still looking into the aquarium. Eva stood next to him and placed her hand on his shoulder, moving her head in front of him, blocking his view.

'Shall we feed him?' she asked mischievously.

'No. Those bugs freak me the fuck out,' he squinted at another cricket that was sat at the other side of the enclosure. He pulled his face away from the box. 'Do you think they know they're being sent to their death?'

'I have a bucket load of them,' Eva replied nonchalantly.

'I don't want to see them,' Oscar said, shuffling his feet together, backing against the radiator. He chucked his cap on the bed in Eva's direction. 'You know I hate bugs, insects, and everything of that ilk.'

'They get out the cage all the time you know. I chase them with tweezers when they do.'

Oscar shuddered. 'Don't. Where do you keep the bucket?'

'In here, look,' Eva opened her cupboard and pulled out a large yellow tub.

'I didn't say get it out, did I?'

'Just have a quick look inside.'

'Honestly. I can't,' Oscar stood on his tip toes and peered over the bed. 'Is the lid securely fastened?' he asked.

Eva continued to stand idly, fixated on the bucket.

'Eva, I know I look like a massive bitch, but I'm telling you, I hate this.'

She put her fingers atop the lid, partially removing it. '*Woah!*' she exclaimed.

Oscar didn't move, but his eyes widened.

'You little shit.'

Eva put the bucket away, her eyes streaming from laughter.

'Go wash your hands! I'm not having roaches or whatever those things are jumping on my dick,' he said impishly, as he hopped onto the bed.

'Oh, you reckon you're getting that?' Eva asked.

'I've never been so sure.'

Eva returned from the bathroom and jumped into Oscar's arms. They embraced and rolled across the bed. They wrapped their tongues together and kissed intensely, breathing down each other's necks as they came up for air. He was fixated on her form with a burning desire, for he loved her so intensely, that the idea of making love to her started to repulse him. She was too precious to be subjected to such depravity. He held her close and stroked her head feverishly. She ran her nails down his back, scratching him tenderly, pulling his moist tee shirt from his head. She kissed his chest before it became too much for him to bear. He pulled her closer, biting her neck playfully and made love to her.

She breathed heavily and pressed her hands against his chest.

'I'm really scared of being loud, I keep thinking my Dad's in.'

He raised her legs, and their souls devoured each other.

It was dark outside, and a gust of wind entered the room. The television was on, and Eva lay still. Her arm rested across Oscar's neck, and her left leg hung over the edge of the bed.

He put his cap back on and reached for the remainder of his beer. A film was playing, but he had missed the start and didn't recognise it, nor did he care, but the sound was calming. He leant across to Eva and wrapped the sheets over her, pulling her leg back onto the bed. He watched her sleep, and when satisfied, kissed her forehead. She said something indecipherable under her breath in a dreary sleep-like manner.

His heart slowed.

He envied Eva's proclivity to collapse into sleep at a moment's notice, and ran his hands across his chest, over the red scratch marks borne from her nails. He rolled behind her, hugging her tightly. He felt uneasy and pressed his form against hers, wrapping his fingers between hers; try as he might, his flesh could not feel the intensity of his love, for no physical sensation held a flame to his enamourment.

His mahogany eyes became heavy, and his shoulders relaxed into the fresh sheets beneath him. He sank into a state of enervation, a dreamlike interlude where abstract shapes and intense colours permeated his mind's eye.

He was woken by the cold grip of the night air. He stood, carefully, and approached the large window to close it, sealing it shut with its plastic handle. Under his foot, a blue light shone dimly from Eva's phone, a small green icon could be seen on it: a message. He rubbed his eyes with his forearm and crouched low to the ground.

It was a message from a recipient named, 'Cubby', that read: 'Good night xx'.

Oscar felt violently sick. He tried to access her phone, but her passcode was no longer the same. His heart thumped loudly.

'What are you doing on my phone.'

Eva looked at him, unmoved from her position, her azure eyes piercing the veil of darkness between them; she was eerily calm.

'Who's Cubby?' asked Oscar.

'A friend.'

'You call your friends Cubby? Is this how friends say goodnight to each other?'

She looked at him insignificantly.

'Like this!' Oscar wrenched the phone forward at Eva's face, stopping only an inch prior to her nose.

She tried to snatch it from his grasp.

'We go to dance class together.'

'Dance class?'

'Pole dancing. He's—gay.'

'Is this what gay guy's do now?' Oscar's knuckles turned a bright white, as his fingers curled round her phone. She remained still, fully composed, and his anger turned to a desperate confusion.

'I'll show you the conversation, pass me my phone,' said Eva.

Oscar proffered the phone to her, his mouth dry and his eyes wide.

Immediately, Eva ripped it from him and darted out of the room, shutting the door behind her; his eyes sought her shadow that chased after her.

He sat on the floor and crossed his legs, pulling his hair over his eyes in the darkness. He waited for her return, feeling as though his organs had been removed.

Not long after, she opened the door and stood before him with her phone outstretched.

'You've just deleted it all haven't you?' asked Oscar.

'You didn't need to see it; you'll just get angry,' replied Eva.

'Why are you giving me your phone if you've deleted it?'

'You can look through it.'

'Are you fucking insane! You've just deleted it?'

She stood solemnly; her hand still outstretched. 'Can you get out of my house please?'

'I'm out of this fucking hell hole!' screamed Oscar.

'Don't ever raise your fucking voice at me in my house! Get the fuck out,' Eva shouted back.

'You're a fucking stupid slut,' Oscar cried.

'Get out.'

'How could you do this to me?' Oscar begged her for an answer, one he did not wish to here.

'I didn't do anything. He's a gay friend. Get the fuck out.'

'Can you not see how that's impossible for me to believe?'

'I don't care, it's the truth. Get out.'

Oscar put his clothes on and grabbed his bag from the closet and dashed out to the street. His head was pounding in confusion, and he tripped over the pavement into a parked car. His shoe flew from his foot, rolling into the road, leaving him nobbled in a fit of tears.

He desperately retrieved it and hobbled to the bench at the end of the road. He sat down, clutching his face, digging his nails into the skin below his tear ducts. He leant forward, pulling his knees into his chest and rocked back and forth. He gasped and wailed at the surrounding emptiness.

'Oscar?'

Eva had approached him in a black cardigan, walking right up beside him. He got to his feet, shaking his head aggressively, letting his tears fall freely.

'Who the fuck do you think you are, leaving my front door open?'

She struck him three times across his temple with a closed fist.

He touched his temple in disbelief and spoke to her in a wobbling voice: 'Why did you do that to me?'

She hit him once more.

'Stop!' he screamed.

She stopped and looked at him; her head cocked to the side as though she was perplexed by his cries.

She raised her fist once more and he spat in her face. She flinched and wiped the spit from her cheek.

'Why did you do that?' she asked, curiously.

'You've just been hitting me! I don't understand?' snot ejected from Oscar's nose, hitting his forearm, his wailing sounding into the night.

The pair looked at each other, as if suspended in time.

Oscar broke the silence, shaking. 'Why are you doing this?'

She looked at him, blinking slowly and thoughtfully.

'Don't ever speak to me again,' said Eva.

She returned to her house, leaving him by the bench. Oscar looked around for a means to kill himself.

He sat, feeling an overwhelming shame. He put his shoe on properly and stifled his tears, whimpering until he had control of his breathing. He looked up to the black sheet of sky above, but the garish glow of the streetlight dazzled him. His head ached and his vision blurred. His mouth tasted salty from the remaining tears that pooled above his top lip.

He remained seated for an hour, and received a text from Eva, stating she was sorry and that she loved him.

He slapped himself across the face, in an attempt to force himself to depart from the bench. From the top of the road, he saw Eva approach once more. He legitimately considered, if this was a fever dream.

'What are you still doing here still? You know I can see you from my window.'

He breathed in deeply. 'I'm about to leave.'
'Why don't you come back in?'
'I can't.'
'If you leave, it's really over this time.'
Oscar was calm, for exhaustion was setting in.
'Do you think you can do better than me?' he asked sparingly.
'Layla thinks I can.'
'I hate Layla.'
'I know you do, and she knows you do,' Eva took her hair bobble out and shook her head gently. 'Are you coming back inside?'
'Probably not.'
'We can't stand in the street?'
'I'm going home.'
'Please come back inside.'
She leant over him, pulling at the back of his arm.
'Don't touch me,' Oscar said with as much spite as he could muster. She continued to pull on his arm.
'I wish you could feel like this,' he told her.
'Please.' She murmured in his ear, her voice gentle and frail.
'I'm leaving, I'll talk to you tomorrow,' he said, ripping his arm free.
'How can you leave me like this? I'm all alone!' Eva screamed under her breath.
'You cheated on me.'
'No, I didn't. I've never cheated on you, and we were on a break anyway.'
Oscar sat back down on the bench, and leant his back against the splintered arm rest, so that he faced her.
'Just come back inside, we can talk inside,' Eva said.
'Too much has happened, hasn't it? It's beyond repair. I don't think I'll ever get over what's been said, it will always eat away at me. I can't trust you…I don't trust you.' Oscar said, gazing down the street.
'I don't need your limp little dick anyway,' Eva said with a still face.
Oscar felt a painful tinge in his heart and looked through the dull glow enveloping him, to the sea of stars above.

'I pray you die, so I can be rid of you. That way, no one else can know you, or have you. I hate what I've become, and I despise you. And in all my hatred for you, I hate myself more, for wanting you, still. You are the single worst thing that has ever happened to me, and I wish with every part of my soul that I could dash your head against the curb.'

Eva paused for a moment.

'But you love me?'

'Of course,' Oscar said, blinking slowly.

'That's not love.'

'Then what is it?' asked Oscar.

'You hate me.'

'I think those two feelings can exist simultaneously.'

'I don't think they can,' Eva said.

'Of course you don't, you're a lizard.'

'I think if you really loved someone, then things would never get to this,' said Eva.

She angled to sit, and Oscar spun his legs to the ground to accommodate her.

'I've been speaking to other people on forums and stuff,' said Eva.

'You've not been on 'forums', you've been on dating apps. A friend told me whilst we were on a break they saw you on there,' Oscar said, pausing for breath between almost every word.

'Which friend was it?'

'Does it matter?'

'I hate your friends, they're such little snakes.'

'What would you prefer he do, not tell me?' asked Oscar.

Her face contorted from anger to boredom.

'If you found a new partner in the future. Would you cheat on them, with me?' asked Eva.

Oscar answered honestly.

'Probably. Would you?'

'I think so.'

They looked at each other's defeated miens.

'Do you want to kiss me?' Eva asked, her brow furrowed.

'There isn't a moment that goes by, that I don't,' Oscar stated.

She shuffled across the bench to him, placing her head on his shoulder.

'I do care for you, but maybe it's best if we don't speak tomorrow.'

He dropped his head against hers, to which she rubbed her cheek against his, their damp flesh adjoining.

'I didn't mean to make you feel like that,' said Eva.

'You did,' said Oscar.

'I didn't. You're such a bright boy. You deserve someone better than me.'

'I don't think I want better.'

'How can you not want better, when that's what you deserve?'

Oscar's eyes began to fill with tears once more.

'Why can't you do it for me?' he pleaded.

'I don't think I can.'

'Why do you tell me you love me all the time, why do you lie to me?'

'It's not a lie. I do.'

'But you said it yourself. This isn't love?'

'I think I have love for you, but I don't want to be with you,' said Eva.

She put her arms round his neck and clasped him tightly. He smelt her sweet scent, mingled with sweat and tears.

'But you'll be with someone else.'

'I won't,' said Eva.

'You will, though. If it's not today, it's tomorrow; if it's not tomorrow, it's the day after,' Oscar said resignedly.

'It will be a long time before I get over you,' said Eva.

'I don't believe that.'

'You don't have to believe me.'

'Fuck's sake,' Oscar cursed himself for his weakness and began to shiver. 'I need to go home.'

'You can stay here.'

'Who would that be good for?' he asked.

'I'd like you to stay here.'
'If I'm staying, I'll stay on the sofa.'
'No, you should stay upstairs with me.'
'No Eva. I'm going to sleep on the sofa.'

They entered the house; Eva locked the door behind them and went to grab him a quilt and a pillow, setting it out on the living room sofa. They said goodnight to each other, and he was left alone. The shutter on the blind was crooked, and the pewter hues of the night pooled into the centre of the room, revealing a cream rug. Oscar lay under the quilt, his feet poking out from beneath it over the end of the sofa. He got back up to shut the door and returned to his post for the night. He listened out for any noises upstairs and heard Eva shut her door and retreat to her bed. He received a message from her shortly after, asking him to come upstairs.

He abandoned his phone to his side. He could hear a grandfather clock ticking away in the hallway and the gentle buzzing of an unknown device in the room with him. He heard Eva turn in her bed upstairs.

Oscar awoke to the sound of Eva's footsteps on the stairs. She opened the door, appearing in front of him in a white dressing gown; her pale blonde hair tied back.

'You should probably block my number—it's really done now.'
'I thought it was really done, before?' asked Oscar curiously.

He lay still, his curled fingers appearing over the top of the blanket.

'I told you it was over if you stayed on the sofa, didn't I? It's done now isn't it.'

He didn't move, but his expression shifted to one of tortured anguish.

'What are you talking about?'
'I clearly said, last night, if you stayed on the sofa, that was it.'
'But you had already ended it, that's why I stayed down here?'
'We could have saved it, if you'd have slept upstairs with me.'

He put his palms over his eyes, blocking out the bewildering figure.

'Am I dreaming?' he asked aloud.

'Get your stuff and get out.'

'Eva, are you being serious?'

'Yes. Get out, I've got a lot to do today.'

'No—not that part. The part about salvaging it'.

'Yeah, dead serious. How can you stay in the same house as your girlfriend and not sleep in the same bed as her?'

'I stayed here for you, so you weren't alone!'

'But I was alone.'

He stood up and attempted to put his arms round her.

'Don't touch me. It's done,' she said sharply.

He caught a reflection of himself in the mirror. His eyes were purple and puffy, and his cheeks were as red as a peach. He dragged his hair across his head and looked at her. Her arms were crossed, and she had the expression of disgust drawn across her face. She looked like her mother.

'Right,' said Oscar.

'Hurry up,' Eva retorted.

'Fuck off you useless bitch.'

She slapped him across the face and squealed at him: 'You're so fucking disgusting.'

He looked at himself once more in the mirror, speaking a soundless proclamation of lacking resolve.

'I'm done.'

'No, I'm done,' said Eva.

'Yeah. I'm done,' Oscar said, again.

Eva walked behind him, pushing him out of the house. He felt some respite as she guided him to the door, for he was awfully tired.

'You always have to have the last word, don't you?'

'Yeah.'

'Just don't say anything.'

'Fuck off.'

'*Don't say anything after me!*' she screamed at the top of her lungs.

She pushed the back of his head, forcing him into the coat room. She took her hands from him, only to unbolt the front door.

'Don't contact me on anything. *Leave!*'

Her hot saliva sprayed across his face, and he walked to the empty driveway in the cold light of day. He winced and slung his bag over his shoulder. He was too exhausted to part with another tear, but after walking some way home, he started bawling.

PART THREE - LIMERENCE

CHAPTER SEVEN

DEFEAT

Two months had passed since their last meeting. And since, Oscar had reached out to Eva multiple times, to no avail. He tried to resist doing so, but the siren's allure was greater than the mariner's resolve.

His mother had departed South again, and he was alone in the house. His dominion slipped from him tenderly. He lay in a bath of cold water and poured a vase of lilies over himself. The dirt married with the water and the white flowers of death floated at his sides; an elegant scent of spice, citrus and earth rising from the tub.

He submerged his head beneath the frigid surface, opening his eyes within the murky waters, his strands of hair weaving with the drowned earth.

He held his breath for as long as he could, until he felt he might burst and rose through the myriads of lilies. He pulled himself out from the basin, the turbid waters of which splashed over to the white bath matt, muddying it. He lay face down on the dirtied matt, his lips pressed up against the muck.

With his first movement from stasis, he dragged himself across the tiles to the radiator. He rose and rubbed a towel generously on his scalp and looked to the bathroom mirror, viewing his features intently, pressing his fingers against the edges of his eyes and pulling at the corners of them. He stretched out his matted curls, so he might loosely measure them; they came to his bottom lip and tasted of dirt.

He trudged to his room, treading filthy water over the landing. He pulled a cream tin out from under his bed. Within, was a pair of clippers that he plugged into a socket atop the stairs. He sat against the landing wall, staining it with the sepia imprint of his back.

He ran the clippers through his hair; tufts of curls floated down and rested on his legs as he scraped his head clean. He thumbed his bald head, running his fingers across the razor thin stubble that now populated his skull. His head looked diminutive, but there was now a shapeliness to it he had never perceived. He held his skull in both of his hands, turning his neck meticulously, uncovering each facet of his head with his fingertips.

He stood upon the bristly remnants which tickled the soles of his feet and plucked his phone from a pile of clothes that lay next to the wash basket.

Richard was calling him.

Oscar looked at his phone and turned it between his fingers, wondering how long the ringing would go on for. He yawned and flexed his toes, waiting for a voice message; he thought it unlikely that one would be left.

He was correct.

He received a text from Richard, informing him that he was driving through the area and would be visiting. He panicked, hastily picking up his abandoned possessions and cleaning up. He hosed himself down under the showerhead and got changed, finishing his ensemble by placing a black cap upon his fleshy scalp.

Soon after, there was a knock at the door. He was already present in the hallway and opened it swiftly. He stared at Richard, who stood against the backdrop of a wintery eve. His friend was dressed in a long navy double breasted coat; his bright hair falling behind his ears. Richard looked at Oscar's face inquisitively.

'Did you go to the barber today?'

'No.'

'Did your Mum do it for you?'

'Yeah, before she went away,' Oscar said, standing aside. 'You want a drink or ote?'

'Go on then. I'm driving though, so I'll just have one.'

'Where's your car?' Oscar asked, looking at the empty drive.

'I had to park down the hill, too many cars blocking the way up.'

The pair walked to the living room, and upon entering, Oscar became confused. The sofa cushions had seemingly escaped the sofas at some unforeseen point in time. He retrieved each of them, fluffing them up before placing them back to their appropriate positions. He then departed to the kitchen, only to return with two bottles of ale.

'Which one do you want?' asked Oscar.

'Any will do.'

'But which one? Because they're both rank.'

'That one,' Richard pointed to the brown ale bottle with the tiger on its label.

Oscar popped the cap and gave it to him, drinking from the other.

'You haven't been answering your phone. Everything alright?' Richard asked, his brow the only visible feature from behind his bottle.

'I've been occupied at the minute.'

'Yeah?'

'Yeah.'

'Have you spoken to Fred since?' asked Richard.

'Nope,' declared Oscar.

'I haven't really, either,' Richard said, cautiously drinking from his bottle.

Oscar set his drink aside, and tried to snatch eye contact with Richard, who remained behind his bottle.

'Actually. I've been meaning to ask you; can you get his dealer's number for me?'

'The Danny Cross guy?' Richard said, tilting his bottle along with his head.

'That's the one.'

'Why?'

'I fancy some weed.'

'Do you think that's a good idea?' Richard probed.

'No,' Oscar said. Thumbing the top of his beer so that it made a popping sound. 'Can you do it anyway?'

'I'll ask.'

'Pretend it's for you though.'

'He won't believe that.'

Oscar walked over to the sofa in front of the window, observing the fabric of the blinds. He sat down here and extended his legs before him, crouching over to pick at his white socks, prolonging the silence.

'What's been happening with Eva?' asked Richard.

'What do you mean?' Oscar replied, nonchalantly.

'Have you seen her recently?'

'I have.'

His friend placed his beer down and cracked his knuckles, as though he might now try to investigate his soul.

'How are you?'

'Yeah, I'm alright.'

'I can get Fran to pick me up later if you want. We can go to the pub?'

'Sure. I have loads of beers in, so we can chill here for a bit beforehand.'

'Sure,' agreed Richard.

The pair traded a glance at one another before looking to their respective bottles.

They finished their drinks and Oscar brought in a half empty box of beers from the outhouse.

'You know Rachel from my Dad's warehouse?' Richard asked.

'I do,' conceded Oscar.

'She was caught stealing loads of cash from the till. Do you remember me saying that my dad put her at the shop? Well, we checked the books and a chunk of money had gone missing over the course of the last few months. She was taking holidays galore as well.'

Oscar raised his eyebrows high above his dead pupils.

'That's insane. Have you sacked her?'

'He's going to speak to her on Monday.'

'But you have footage? or just the info from the books,' asked Oscar.

'Just the books, but it's evidence enough. She was the only one working at the time the cash was taken.'

'Interesting,' Oscar said unconvincingly, finishing his beer. He thought to offer Richard another, but his friend was still lapping at the foam atop his bottle. So, he remained silent and reached for another.

'So, are you seeing Eva over the weekend at all?' asked Richard.

'Probably not, we've had a bit of an argument recently.'

'Oh right. Bad one?'

Oscar popped the cap off his ale with his back tooth and watched the seal spring out from his mouth and skitter across the floor.

'Have you tried to talk to her since?' pursued Richard.

'Not really,' said Oscar.

'Do you think you'll get back together?'

'I don't fucking know,' Oscar sighed, crushing his eyelids together to avoid resorting to tears, sheltering his actions behind the brim of his cap.

'How's Fran?' he asked abstrusely through a mouth of beer.

'She's good. Well, I say that. She's had to go to the hospital recently; in and out.'

'Why?'

'It's just lady problems.'

'Is she on antibiotics or anything, have they sorted her out?'

'She's been prescribed something. Hopefully she'll feel better with them.'

Richard caught up to Oscar, finishing his drink. Oscar nudged the crate with his foot, to which Richard dipped his hand into.

'Do you want a spirit or anything, instead? I think there's half a bottle in the back.'

'We should probably stick with this,' Richard chuckled, tapping the top of his bottle with his nail.

'What's the difference, it's all poison,' said Oscar.

Richard shuffled back as far as he might into his seat and pulled out his phone.

'Do you think I'm being off or something?' Oscar asked compellingly.

'No. But I've been concerned. After what happened, you haven't been picking up your phone or replying to me—it's been ages.'

'I'm sorry,' Oscar said, overwhelmed by a tinge of sadness.

'It's okay.'

'It's not okay, I shouldn't have neglected you. I'm sorry.'

'You've said sorry, it's okay,' said Richard.

'I'm just not all there at the minute, really.'

'There with what?'

'I'm just not.'

Oscar cleared his throat, tapping his feet on the wooden floor.

'Do you want to head out now?' asked Richard.

'It's cold out, isn't it? I best put some layers on.'

Oscar dragged himself upstairs to his wardrobe. His room was cold, and dusty strands of web hung from the ceiling. He wondered if these webs would ever fall on him as he slept, or if they would remain in place, forever.

From his wardrobe, he pulled out a black sheepskin coat adorned with a furred collar. He had never worn it before but was drawn to it. He trudged to the bathroom, viewing himself whilst donning the coat. He pulled his hat off and gazed at his pale head; his skull retreated into the black furry mass of his collar, and he became fearful of his countenance as he stared into his dark eyes, ruminating under the pallid bathroom light. He put his cap back on and returned downstairs.

He saw Richard standing by the door on his descent, eager to leave.

'You're not going to finish your beer?' Oscar asked, throwing his arms up from his sides.

'Nah, I'll just get another one out.'

Oscar retrieved a last beer from the crate and shut the living room door behind him.

The pair departed. Little was said as they ventured up the road. The eve was pitch black and the air smelt of winter decay. The pavements were laden with frost, and the branches of the dying trees were touched by snow. Icy flakes billowed gently above them, melting instantly on contact with their warmth. Their breath turned to vapour, misting before them. Oscar pulled out a pair of dark leather gloves from the bottom of his coat pocket.

'Where did you get those?'

'I don't know! Cool though, right? They must have been my Grandad's.'

Richard jerked his head to the glove, as though he was existentially disturbed by it, causing him to stumble from the curb to the road, slipping on an invisible sheet of black ice. Oscar grabbed his friend's arm to steady him, and in doing so, he too, was almost felled. The pair shared a bitter smile.

They arrived at the centre of the darkening suburb and stood outside the golden hearth. The snow had ceased, and a milling crowd blocked their way.

'I'll grab us a drink.' Richard declared.

'You sure?' Oscar looked at the thrashing mass of extremities and heads before them.

'Yeah, don't worry about it. Do you want to find us somewhere to sit?'

Oscar's vision failed to penetrate the crowd; people stood all the way to the entrance.

'It's going to have to be an outside job.'

With this, he made his way through the crowd; the emitted warmth of which was equal parts isolating and comforting. He Sighted a small table towards the perimeter, pushed up against a bed of dead flowers and an adjoining building. He pushed past the undirected mass of bodies and lay claim to the table, placing his knee atop the bench as he scoured the vicinity. He placed his gloved hands together on the table and sighted a series of familiar faces. Some greeted him, some did not. Some tried to sit with him, some did not. The visitors were both good and bad, because there are none who are wholly good, and none who are wholly bad.

Richard soon returned through the crowd, carrying two rimy glasses to the table. Bronze liquor spilled over from them as he pivoted past the bystanders and onlookers. He placed a glass before Oscar, sitting next to him.

'Cheers,' they said in unison, clinking their glasses together, the fluid spilling onto their coats.

They raised their voices significantly to speak, the dinning sounds of the public serving only to thwart them.

'Do you think Fred will be here tonight?' Richard asked.

'Probably not. He doesn't leave his local does he, unless he's seized from it.'

'True.'

'He's the least of my worries,' said Oscar.

'Do you think he's harmless?' Richard asked.

'I don't think anyone is.'

The pair drank earnestly, awash with all manner of chatter that follows intoxication.

Through the gap between the wall and the crowd, above the flower beds to his left, Oscar sighted a figure that resembled Eva, crossing the road opposite The Admiral.

He leaned his back against the wall, scrupulously looking through the gap for clarification; it was clearly her. She was dressed in all black, decorated in a large overbearing jumper, the sleeves of which, fell to the tips of her fingers. Her makeup was dark, and her face was light. He now realised his initial apprehension was only due to the new colour of her hair, which was a rich brown. Her dark locks fell over her shoulders, untethered, spilling across her neck, bobbing with every stride she took.

She was not alone.

Oscar pulled his defeated eyes away from the scene. He placed his head on the table in a puddle of beer and turned his neck to look out to the crowd, exhaling a sound of quiet desperation. He soon realised the strange sight which had befallen Richard, and plucked his head up, choosing instead to rest his chin on the rim of his glass.

Richard spat a laugh at him.

'Alright?'

'I'm not.'

'What's up?'

'I've just seen Eva with someone.'

'How do you know they're together?'

'He had his hand on her back.'

'That doesn't mean they're together?'

Oscar's tongue stiffened and he felt a sickening rush of adrenaline course through him.

'Lower back.'

Richard muttered something under his breath, but Oscar couldn't hear it. His ears were ringing, and his cheeks flushed a pale blue.

'Do we know him?' Richard asked.

'Sort of.'

'Who is it?'

Oscar looked down, almost wanting to laugh.

'Red.'

Richard remained hushed.

Oscar cupped his ears, blocking out the surrounding cacophony. He leant back on the bench, so that he might rest his head against the wall. He looked at the splendour of the night sky above and saw the stars dance to the sound of a cosmic joke.

'He's not in prison then.'

'Guess not,' said Oscar.

'Do you want to leave?'

'I'm alright.'

They finished their drinks. Oscar passed Richard his debit card; the card attached to his savings account.

'Just grab us whatever.'

'Are you sure? I'll just get us a couple of pints, so I don't have to requeue.'

'I don't mind.'

'What's the pin?'

'Six, one, seven, four,' said Oscar.

Richard departed, making his way in a leisurely fashion through the swathes of people.

Oscar ripped off his gloves, stuffing them into his coat pocket and whipped out his phone, pulling up Eva's contact. He typed furiously, his heart skipping and palpitating within the walls of his ribcage. His fingers lingered on the screen as he deleted and reformatted his message multiple times. Words were futile, but nevertheless, all that he had.

Upon texting her, he put his phone away and yanked his gloves back over his hands, wrestling them up his wrists. He clutched the brim of his cap, forcing it down as tightly on his head as it would go. He folded his arms, tapping his foot on the stone floor incessantly. His jaw clamped and his teeth gritted together violently; he dug his gloved fingers deep within his right palm, hoping to prise it open so that he be covered in hot blood. He pushed his shin deep into the wooden leg of the table until he winced, but did not pull it away, for the pain only added cause to embed it further. He hoped by some turn of fate it would saw his leg off.

'You've got a lot to say for yourself haven't you!'

A voice rippled through the night air, cutting through the racket. A semblance of silence formed after, which soon transformed into the breathy murmurs of those surrounding him. He could not see the man who had bellowed these words, but he was sure of the culprit. He shrugged, looking to the ground so he may collect his thoughts, capturing each of them before they escaped him.

A flutter of excitement almost served to lift him from his chair, but an appropriation of fear kept him down. What was to come of this? The scenarios that perturbed him did little to paint a picture of any real outcome that may be birthed. The crowd was yet to part and his accuser remained covered by bodies. He looked for Richard, with the understanding his friend could provide a reliable sheath to the situation, preventing it from descending into outright chaos. But now, chaos was his God.

The crowd had still not parted, and he knew it to be only a matter of time until the figure emerged. He considered rushing through the crowd, in a gambit to stupefy the accuser. However, the swaying crowd looked sure to not budge. And an action like this, may even be seen by the crowd, as an awkward escapade, or even a failed escape.

He heard the voice once more but could not make out what was said. Although, it seemed that the crowd had heard these words, as their murmurs fell silent once more and their faces appeared sincere. This caused much consternation within him, and he fiddled with his gloves again, pulling them halfway up his hands, only to then drag them back down his wrists. The next object of his parley was his hat. It would be mortifying if a fight were to break out, and his hat were to become a victim of the scuffle. His gloves, at the least, provided him with an illusion of readiness, whereas his hat did not. He decided it best if he bundled it into his boxer shorts. Here, was the only haven for such things, as there was ample space for the possession to be clasped against the rear of his buttock; it did not fit in his pockets, nor anywhere else, and at the least, it would not be lost to the crowd. He winced at the prospect of his hat becoming a bloody memento that might be carried across the sea of hands, only to be pocketed by some bum. This was the worst-case scenario, not for himself, but for his belongings. His phone and wallet were buried in the depths of his pockets as far down as they would go; they should be safe.

'Where you at!' The voice sounded again, and this time, Oscar could hear it clearly amidst the soft sounds of trainers and boots that twisted against the stone ground.

A myriad of eager eyes searched the seats for a name, any name. The crowd started to jeer airily, carrying now, a hint of impatience. The prospect of exhilaration fading before the horde with every passing moment.

'Let's leave, come on.'

It was Eva's voice emanating from the quiet chatter; how could it not be? The hurried intonation and the grating but sweet tone. This revelation fueled Oscar with a call from the beyond. He rose to his feet and slapped himself gently against his cheek. The stakes were now dramatically raised. If she was not present, at least two stories would make their way to her. Now, there was only one naked truth that could be surmised. A glaring cold, objective verity. He calmed himself, for there was only one predestined outcome already written across the constellations. He simply had to play his part, and what a part that might be, he mused.

His thoughts rose incessantly as he primed his body for pain. He hoped to land a punch so convincing; so persuasive, so deafening, that it would, by its own merit create an almighty ruckus, alerting a bouncer inside The Admiral. He knew this to be a pipe dream, in truth, he knew he would have to survive for a great deal of time, even longer than he might anticipate.

He did not speak, as to not confirm his presence to the crowd and what lay beyond. Instead, he walked forth. The crowd looked to him as he moved, as though they were symbiotically alerted to his presence. They had found their combatant in him. Words and jibes were directed to him, and some scoffed, while others were pleasantly surprised, and many were too drunk to think.

He hoped to delay the encounter, for the longer tension could build, the more he could save face. And perhaps, the more apprehensive he would make Eva's courter. He trusted that Eva would not wish to demean him after this event and prayed that the information passed on to Red if any, would be limited. Or, at least, as limited as one might decide—or important enough to warrant speaking of a previous lover.

He was now in danger of appearing meagre to the masses before him. He did not wish for this festivity to turn into a sacrifice, one that surely would, if he were to not approach soon. He pressed his sheepskin coat down neatly with the square of his hands. Although he felt fatigue and dizziness, his legs and footing were solid and did not give out on him. He put this strange feeling down to the mingling of drink and adrenaline; a concoction of deep regret.

He walked up to the first layer of the crowd which peeled back before him, revealing another line of jeering folk. Some of them, he knew, but more as a footnote in his life which marked a particular day, or instance. One that was so far from him, an erasure of such would carry no meaning. Someone spoke to him hurriedly as he passed, but he could hear naught. His ears were ringing with tinnitus, spurred by the heat of battle. He almost forgot of Eva and his plight in this moment; the ringing noises did little to remind him of this, and acted only, to ground him in viscerality.

He was pushed forward into a crowded circle. There was little hope of escape here, for even a rat would have its share of trouble; a rodent would not be able to weave and entwine its form around this many surrounding feet.

Eva stood before him. She was backed up against the crowd, as a white ghost beneath her umber hair. She was neither wholly ahead of the crowd, nor within it. She existed in flux, between the blurred line of spectator and partaker, contending with the pushing and bustling. Her eye met his, and she struck him a look of concern, fear, anguish and euphoria. Her maddened eyes were most becoming of her.

Ahead of her, Red Stood. He looked indignantly at Oscar's eyes, retraining them on his presence.

'You've got a lot to say for yourself. Haven't you?'

Oscar looked up at Red; he was identical to their last meeting, which now existed to him as a blur in the depths of his memory. He wondered if the man had remembered him from this chance encounter, or, if he simply did not care. Meeting people held little weight; they were always too keen to cast aside what little rapport they had built in the face of a greater occasion.

Oscar remained silent.

Red had one of those faces that you could not see failing him, even if it were to be hit by a truck. His skull was set low, and his cheekbones, high and raised. His neck carried the vast load of his skull and was naturally hunched. The corners of his black stubbled hair disappeared into the reaches of his scalp. From where Oscar stood, he could not determine how far they went back. But he was surprised that the ridge of their brows almost met, and he could not tell if this was due to the figure's hunched demeanor, or, if the height of Red's brawny frame played tricks on his eyes.

He continued to hold the man's gaze, waiting for the crowd to quieten, or for something else to happen. He dared not look back to Eva, who he could see at his peripheral for concern of igniting Red's latent anger. He could not remain in this position of stasis for much longer, for fear of losing face.

The crowd was lulled into an amicable state, swinging gently in the cold night air. All was well within the audience, and their hunger would soon be satiated.

'What I said, wasn't for you,' answered Oscar.

'You think she's not going to tell me?' Red scorned.

Oscar afforded Eva a disappointed look, one that he did not have time to see reciprocated, as Red stepped closer, blocking his vision. The only thing that stopped their lips from meeting was their noses. There was no compromise to be found, or had, and escalation was inevitable. Oscar knew if he were to initiate, it would look poor. There was little chance Red could be taken down with a single swing, and by then, the man would have surely clambered atop him. At the least, he was primed as the victim. There was nothing admirable in this, but sympathy was his only ally; a pathetic, sickening one, but an ally, nonetheless. In times of war, people do well to not be choosy, he thought.

He considered wrestling with Red, bringing him to ground. This was possible, but the outcome of such would see Red on top of him, again, concluding in him being pounded into the stone floor. He could not see himself maneuvering atop the burly specimen if they fell. He thought again of using the crowd as leverage to prevent a fall, perhaps he could then twist Red into their bodies, landing something meaningful before colliding to ground. Hoping then, that the crowd would provide enough distance between them, for him to recuperate for a second volley.

Oscar stood, facing the crowd, but he could not see Eva, nor were the same faces present in front of him. Confused, he looked at the heads of the crowd, which twisted and writhed as a single mass. Their serpentine faces contorted into expressions of awe and fear, their mouths agape and their hair on end. Oscar felt a hot substance trickle down his temple, congealing in the cold and cascading to the floor by his foot. The red tear splattered against the stone pavement and his shoe. He checked his hand, which was now trembling profusely, but undamaged. His phone was on the ground before him, and his wallet, alongside its contents, was strewn across the ground. He wished to retrieve his items, but was perplexed, insurmountably confused by the position in which he stood, and why he was bleeding. A dull ache rose from his lower neck and a cramping prevailed from it, stiffening his being.

Screams came from the crowd, some of the audience in disbelief, others in bewilderment, but all in conformity. Their cacophonous chanting drew from him almost all his will.

He turned to face Eva, whose countenance was stricken a grieving white. The lurid purple of the night sky was the only sight of reprieve; for his eyes danced from one hellish sight to the next.

Now, Red stood before him, with what he could only assume as his blood covering the man's mitt.

He tried to muster enough ferocity to return something to Red's jaw, but it was more performative than anything else. He landed his punch, and felt one returned to him, straight and true, puncturing his lips and smashing his teeth. The connection, although less dastardly than the one that had seen him spin in a state of confusion; leaving him unconscious on his feet, was still exceptionally painful.

Oscar felt a searing pain well up in his nose and his remaining enthusiasm waned. He caught himself against the ebbing wave of the crowd that encroached on him, gripping the arm of someone behind him, covering them in blood. His hold was jerked away from him, and he had little alternative, but to try tackle Red. Perhaps only then, would he make it through this.

Still, he thought it a miracle he remained, stood. Part of him wished that Red's first punch would have ended him, indefinitely. Alas, that was not to be, and he must endure. His black coat was now covered in hues of browns and maroons, and on this cold night, did sweat and blood flow.

He narrowly ducked under another vicious swing and managed to bundle his arms around Red's neck. To his surprise and relief, his weight was enough to topple his foe. The pair tumbled to the earth, flurrying relentlessly as they entangled. Red's knee crushed Oscar's testicles, knocking all the air out of his lungs and winding him. He almost feinted from the ensuing nausea and, if it were not for this predicament, surely would have.

Red trapped him under his uncanny weight, pressing his forearms into his chin. He lurched his head from side to side under the hold, trying to bite at Red's ear, but he could not find purchase with his teeth. Instead, he opted to try to strangle the man. His eyes were lit with menace and despair, and his teeth gleamed a wicked red under the electric light of the prevailing streetlamp. He dug the nails of his thumbs into Red's neck, pleading with his hands to commit murder. Yet, this only served to provoke Red, who responded with a surge of punches, leaving him almost unconscious. His vision doubled and his ears rang deafeningly.

He was being pummeled and there was little he could do. He turned his head as Red worked his kidneys with his fists and saw the white faces of the crowd turn to the colour of periwinkle.

Red was no longer atop him, and the striking pains had stopped. He lay still, craning his neck to the side, allowing him to see over his rising and falling chest. He could no longer see Red, and the crowd had since taken some steps back. He looked for Eva and saw her standing just ahead of the crowd; still and shy. He looked at her sad and searchingly. She returned a look that signaled disgust and sympathy, as though she had just witnessed a display of somber incompetence from someone who only existed in her distant memory—an affiliation one holds with someone they met at an inopportune time. Disdainfully, she turned, and Oscar saw her nubile form sway in her clinging black attire.

He was unsure of how much time had passed. Pain presented itself to him separately from delirium. The two feelings were not inextricably bound; one tended to depart as the other arrived. Considering this, he prepped himself for the waves accordingly. Though initially he was uncertain if he was paralysed, he soon understood the sensations to be more akin to sleep paralysis. He could still move his limbs, but it demanded great effort to do so.

He craned his neck forth and scanned ahead of him, realising the crowd had moved further back. One of his eyes felt significantly larger than the other, which was of great concern to him, even in this defeated position.

Seemingly guided by a gust of fresh air that washed over him, he rose and retrieved his belongings, steadying himself against a table corner. He pulled his cap out from the back of his boxer shorts and donned it. His pale fingers were covered in speckles of blood, and he reached to his nose, running his finger over a crooked bump that now extended from its bridge. His breathing had since felt difficult, and he realised one of his nasal passages had collapsed inward.

He looked around, staving off his confusion with the sobering realisation of defeat. This was as good as any demise, or worse than. None approached him, but he empathised with those in his surroundings. He thought he might do the same if he were them.

He made his way out of the premises and hobbled away from the scene, marching up the hill back to his abode. Only stopping behind the wall of a Chinese restaurant, to throw up horrifically. What he expelled, could only be described as a mixture of blood, mucous and bile. The malodorous stench subdued him, and he managed to make his way home with minimal difficulty.

He stumbled over the living room floor, spilling his possessions beneath him. Only then, did he allow himself to crumple into a depressing heap. He cried tears of regret, as one would if they were to bear the brunt of crushingly sad news for eternity.

The night ensued, and so did his utter desolation. He checked his phone with some effort, and to his rue, saw a notification pertaining to two missed calls from Richard, but none from Eva. He made his way upstairs, walking over the dried muck atop the landing and undressed feverishly. He lay on his bed and let his blood tarnish his white sheets.

He dared not visit the bathroom, as then, he would have to look at the mirror, and he feared he would hate his reflection more than he could possibly conceive.

He tried to call Eva but was met with nothing. He was sure she had blocked his number, so he pulled up her email address, and wrote a passage of sickening contemplation. He wished that some invisible force might pull him away from doing such, but there was no such spectre to aid him.

He pleaded with her, and asked for truths he did not wish to here. He pontificated on her betrayal, and if she thought he truly deserved to experience all he did.

To his surprise, a reply was sent back to him almost immediately. He looked over the email with watery red eyes. He was met with some abuse, and some indignation. But his eyes were averted to one part, where Eva claimed, that since they had separated, the sex was far better with other men.

Despite his physical trauma, there was no strike that Red had landed, or feeling that panged with such an intensity, as Eva's sobering words.

He grew from his bed, standing straight and tall by his door. He thought he might withstand the shock, but was immediately met with a strange feeling, as if someone had sprinted up behind him and kicked him in the back of his leg, causing him to lose all strength. It was a surreal sensation. He became flush with a white heat and started sweating profusely. He steadied himself by pushing his back against the door, sliding down it. There was not a chance he could stand and contemplate such news; he was forced from his feet to the floor and was unsure if a weight had been lifted from his psyche, or a permanent indent had been cast upon it. There was a lightness to his breathing, and a lucidity to his mind that had not existed previously. He soon realised that this respite was only momentary, and another pang of pain blossomed in his breast, evolving into one of outright torment. He considered if he was going to die, if his heart had finally cracked in two. But it was not a pain that manifested in a serious way. Instead, it sat upon him, as a house cat does upon one's chest. Inconveniencing him, but not in a way that caused him further distress, for he may not have an opportunity to feel its presence again.

He rested against the wall, acknowledging there was little more he could say to Eva. He had underestimated the desperation of his situation. There were many who had now felt her touch, and many who had done so in a way that encouraged more praise than he had ever received. Even amidst this horror, he was distraught, as he still craved for her to be seated alongside him. He rocked between fits of rage and outbursts of deep sadness. He thought to let himself mourn, but that would pertain to her premature death in his mind.

He reflected on his fight, if he were to call it that. There were solutions that presented themselves in hindsight, as with the nature of all recollections. But he would have done naught differently, for there was nothing to do differently. He decided it best if he were to sleep until morning, but the fog of despair only thickened when he lay in bed.

At no point in his email did he enquire Eva for carnal knowledge. He had specifically formulated his questioning in a way that provoked condolence, or at the least, solicitude. Why would she hurt him in this way? There was no cause to do such, and there was no impending necessity to do so, either. He wanted nothing more than numbing lies, and, after all, did his predicament not warrant this? Was he not to be afforded such comforts as he lay, bleeding out in his own home, not least from the one who had shared her being and loins with him, intimately?

If he was to have his commiserations castrated, why were they to be severed by the one he loved so dearly. His torment was not directed at Red, for Red was only playing a part. Eva would surely have found some other useless reprobate to accompany her, if not him, he thought.

He cursed aloud, blood gargling from his mouth. He hoped for an intruder to trudge up the stairs, on the grounds of something that resembled an armed robbery, to find him sprawled against the wall of the landing. He wished then that the intruder was armed and would proceed to pull out a long-silenced pistol, placing its muzzle against his dying flesh between his eyes, putting a bullet there. Only then, would the blitz on his psyche cease. He pictured Eva in the throes of pleasure with other men, their hands prising her clothes from her form and thrusting their members deep into her, her face curled in ecstasy.

His mouth was hot with saliva, and he felt as though his organs had been removed and rearranged inside him. He struck his large eye forcefully with the palm of his hand and felt a splitting headache form at the pit of his skull.

He rang Richard, who picked up slower than he would have liked.

'Oscar! What happened? Someone said you got attacked...I tried to ring you?'

'It was sort of my fault,' Oscar conceded.

'What do you mean?'

He cast his eyes down to his fingers, which he twisted together in a shape that loosely resembled horns protruding from his knuckles.

'They're probably exaggerating. It wasn't that bad.'

'I'll come over now if you want? I'm on the way back with Fran, but we can turn round?'

'Nah. It's not that big of a deal, it was just a tussle.'

'Are you sure?'

'No, I'm not sure. I'm bleeding out on my stairs, can you come?'

Muttering ensued on the other end of the line. He couldn't make out what was said, but he had an idea.

'We're coming now,' said Richard.

'I'm just messing with you—don't bother. I was going to ask you for something but won't whilst Fran can hear me. I'll text you instead.'

He knew this would incite much hostility between the couple.

'Okay, text me,' replied Richard.

He hung up and placed his phone gently on his lap. He turned to his left to look at the dark interior of his room. His eyes searched for the object of his desire on the shelf, and with great effort made his way to it.

He stepped on the mattress on the floor, and, now elevated, reached for a black folder that sat on the top shelf. From which, he drew a crumpled, yet intact piece of paper. He looked at the paper, reading a sentence from it, before placing it on his bedside table. He was concerned it may be lifted from the table by an invisible gust of air, never to be seen again, so he placed a cup atop it, clamping it to the nightstand.

He texted Richard, following up on the number for Danny Cross, in the hope it had made its way down the grapevine from Fred. It would be a shame for his plan to be foiled at the first hurdle. But, shortly after, Richard replied with the number, followed by a questioning of Oscar's intent.

He texted Danny's number, introducing himself as Fred's friend, stating that they had met before.

His phone rang.

'Hello.'

A gritty voice sounded, 'How did you get my number?'

Unsure if his previous message had been ignored, or if this was just a strange etiquette, he chose to repeat the contents of his message.

'I'm Fred's mate, we've met before?'

'I meet a lot of people.'

'I've no doubt you do,' Oscar replied hesitantly.

There was heavy breathing on the other end of the line.

'What do you want?' Danny asked.

'What have you got?'

'Almost anything.'

'Gun?' Oscar asked.

The heavy breathing stopped.

'Why do you need that?'

'For my protection,' said Oscar.

'What do you need protection from, in Kellwell?'

'Is it something you can do?' asked Oscar, imperatively.

'Take your SIM card out and destroy it. Then, destroy your phone and make a note of the number I'm about to send you; only message it from a new phone.'

'How much?'

'Two bags.'

'Grand?'

'Yeah.'

'So that's all I need to do?'

Danny hung up, leaving him to bathe in the ambient light of his screen. Immediately, a number came through. He scribbled it on a piece of paper, shoved the note through a crack in one of his drawers, and went to bed.

PART THREE - LIMERENCE

CHAPTER EIGHT

DIVINE RETRIBUTION

Oscar awoke and the lands were awash with mist. His window had remained open through the night, but he could not remember opening it. Whisps of fog encroached on his solitude, as he lay at mercy to the day.

He walked to the shower naked, catching a glimpse of himself in the bathroom mirror. His stubbled hair stood on his head like a reddened crown, and streaks of blood had dried and crusted over his face, creating an infernal appearance. His body was in agony, but it was a dull agony, one he felt would ease as the day progressed.

After showering, he looked through the contents of his wardrobe and found a plum-coloured top he had only worn a handful of times earlier in his adolescent years; it still fit him perfectly. He also retrieved a pair of black jeans, a black hooded top and a cap. Once changed, he removed the SIM card from his phone, and snapped it between two of his fingers without deliberation, he then proceeded to crush his phone between his bedroom window and the windowsill, slamming the window shut repeatedly until his phone was ruined.

He retrieved the annotated note from his drawer and placed it in his wallet. He thought it best to hydrate, and poured a glass of water in the kitchen, before another, and then a third, sliding the glass across the sink as he departed.

Passing back through the dining room, his torso grazed against his mother's white lilies, which hung from the olive-coloured vase on the table. The vase was teetering on the edge of which, and the lilies peered over to the floor. He pushed the vase back to the center of the bench, covering himself in more pollen. He felt a tingling sensation in his nose, hoping dearly he would not have an allergic reaction; he bit down on his teeth, and the sensation passed.

Try as he might, he could not remember moving the vase to the edge of the table, and if he did move it last night, surely, he would have brushed against the flowers on the way to the kitchen when entering? He rubbed the golden pollen into his pullover until it was no longer visible.

With no further delay, he exited the house on the hill and walked to the town centre, arriving at his destination.

He walked through the revolving doors of the bank and marched straight to the first teller he sighted, who was positioned behind a glass window nearest the entrance. Her face was large and affable, and her expression held the same endearment as one would have supposed from her features. Yet, when Oscar approached, her expression changed to one of concern. In his haste, he had forgotten that he had two black eyes, and a score of bruises across his face.

He tried to alleviate the taut silence by greeting the teller with a polite smile. Thankfully, this gave her just reason to compose herself, making her retreat into character.

'Good morning sir. How can I help you?'.

'You all good?'

'I'm good. How can I help you?'.

'I'm here to withdraw some cash.'

'How much, exactly?'

'Let's say two grand—wait…Can we make it two thousand, one hundred?'

He handed the teller his card and his provisional driving license.

'From your savings account, is this correct?

'Correct,' said Oscar.

'For security purposes, we have to ask you what you require the money for?'

'I'm looking to purchase a car, in cash.'

The teller asked a variety of security questions before conceding; handing him the exact amount in notes. Oscar winced in pain as he thanked her and left, skulking under his hood to the exit.

Next, he went to Kellwell's closest thing to a phone shop, which was more of a second-hand shop for computer accoutrements. He visited the phone aisle and plucked from it the cheapest prepaid mobile he could find. When paying, the interaction played out in much the same fashion as the one at the bank, with an initial call for platitude being cast by Oscar, before a retreat from the clerk's subversion was made.

With a sigh he retreated home.

He sat on his bed idling. His shoes present upon his stained sheets.

When his new phone was setup and in working order, he withdrew the note from his wallet and messaged the number. His head was sore and heavy, and his eyes weary. He drifted further from consciousness, feeling the mortal coil of his being loosen. He exerted only as much will as needed to remain awake; jerking his head forward each time it drifted backwards and each time his eyes and mind failed him.

He looked through the window to the fog. The mists blurred his view ahead to the rest of the sleepy suburban homes. He imagined beyond, lay green pastures that rolled on, endlessly.

He was uncertain if he had drifted off; his eyes reopened to one of his legs hanging off the bed stretching towards the door, as though it refused to be a part of his being any longer. He sighted his phone, which had fallen atop his heart. He had still not received a reply from the number, and sat up, arching his wounded torso over his phone, cocking his eyes wide open.

He rang the number, letting it ring six times before hanging up. He tried a second time, and finally, a third, wondering if his gambit was too daring, after all.

The call connected, and he was met with a strange disquiet. He waited before speaking; in the vague hope that the recipient would be the first to appraise their acquaintance.

He hesitated, a part of him now hoped the silent recipient would tire of this delay and hang up, rendering his crazed plan useless. Then, he could pretend none of this had ever taken place, so he might return to the norm. Would this not be a true victory? To live in such suffering, and to not find meaning within it, but to instead find a fitting confinement place which held his form perfectly, enveloping every inch of him. Securing him of all woes and minacious thoughts, shielding him of all potential bleak ventures and outright failings. Could this ever be attained? If it were possible, surely it would have become apparent by now? And if it ever had, he was not to know.

A voice sounded from the phone.

'Oscar?'

He was taken aback. For one, that his name was spoken, and second, at the polite inquiring tone of the voice. He was unsure if this was due to the antiquity of the phone; bringing the middle frequencies of the stranger's voice forth, or if it this was the man's authentic sound. If so, he sounded faraway, but intimately close all the same. His tone was fair and bright, a spirit in the machine.

'Hello,' said Oscar

'I have been made aware; you want to buy a gun?' the stranger asked.

'Yes,' declared Oscar.

'Can I ask you a question?' the stranger continued.

'Go on.'

'Is this your choice alone, is this of your agency? It is very important, that it is. I cannot help you if not. Surely you of all people understand this?'

'I do,' Oscar concurred.

'Good. I will not inquire as to what you are using the weapon for. That is not of any concern to me. My abjection might only come from your soundness of mind. If you are not sound of mind, I refuse to sell to you.'

Oscar grew concerned, the fingers of his free hand flexed in pain as his knuckles cracked; the cracking sounded like a chain of falling domino bricks.

'This is entirely my decision,' said Oscar.

'I would like to meet you at the junction, some way out of Kellwell. When you pass the cathedral in the town centre, walk down the road leading South until you arrive at an intersection.'

Oscar thought to ask what he would be looking for upon arrival, but the stranger's tone put him at no doubt of the man's disposition.

'When?' Oscar asked.

'Now.'

The stranger remained on the line and Oscar was unsure whether to wait until the man hung up, though he felt in no uncertain terms that the man would remain on the call, perpetually.

He ended the call, and remained where he was positioned, at the edge of a crumbling precipice which gave way to a swirling oblivion.

He left his home and descended into town. The fog was ever present outside, and the lactescent glow of shop lights did little to pierce the mists. He arrived at the graveyard at the foot of the cathedral. The bell chimed a haunting sound across the town loudly, but the sound was not unkind to the ear, for it had a comforting melodious quality to it.

He stood in the mist, reminding himself that it was the Southern Road exiting from the grounds he must take. The bell continued to chime; he wondered if there was a small figure up there in the roof of the cathedral, pulling at ropes, or some other manner of device that rang the bell. He was uncertain if these days a newer technology was used to ring it, rendering this enigmatic figure's job redundant.

'You look troubled.'

The words came from a man who had taken up residence beside him. The voice was from a priest, who wore a black robe with a clerical collar, and had a white scruffy mane with large spectacles, lending themselves more to the aesthetic of the comic than the sincere. The priest's gruff hand hesitantly remained in the thick of the fog; he looked unsure whether to clasp Oscar's shoulder in a form of consolation or reprisal.

Oscar did not see, or hear the priest approach, but this mattered little, for he was in the stomping grounds of such a man.

'Troubled?' Oscar asked curiously.

The priest allowed his nature to inform his decision, and moved his levitating hand to Oscar, clasping his shoulder.

'Yes. Troubled.'

Oscar cast his vision through the mist to the man's countenance. He saw the crumpled smile and the folded hooded eyes of the priest, which were both dark and bright. Two mild-mannered white brows framed his face, and his nose and ears were bulbous. When he smiled, his eyes disappeared under his eyelids and a missing tooth was revealed between his chapped lips.

Oscar was so displaced by the priest's performance, he almost laughed, and smiled back at the man

'Can I help you?' said the priest.

'No, I'm fine, I'm just passing through,' replied Oscar.

'Not with directions. Is there anything you wish to speak about?'

Oscar remained inert; the priest still gripped his shoulder, but this gave the man of God no power to draw any information from him.

'I lost my wife recently. She was my best friend, a dear creature. She is impossible to replace, nor would I ever try,' said the priest.

'I'm sorry to hear that.' Oscar said, more out of formality than concern. But all the while, he felt a tinge of regret in his heart.

'I look to meet her again one day, but I have much to do here still—I think, or I hope.'

The Priest offered Oscar a dejected smile, and his eyes drifted around the graveyard searchingly, as though he might see his wife once more, walking across the grounds.

'Sixty years we were together—No! sixty-one, as of next week. We met at school; can you believe it? We married as soon as we could afford to.'

The priest looked to Oscar, still beaming, but his eyes were devoid of comfort, and his expression echoed melancholy.

Lilies Of The Damned

'Where are you off to? Have you ever considered visiting the church? Even if you do not wish to sit in with us, it is a grand design, isn't it?'

The priest motioned to the church, although Oscar was unsure what the question truly entailed. He looked up to the impenetrable sky, overcast perennially; through the moving mists above he could make out the gnarled fingers of the spires.

'It is,' Oscar agreed, flatly.

The Priest looked to him with a desperate face of concern. He felt the old man's hand tremble atop his shoulder.

'Go home. Please.'

The sadness in the priest's voice was so profound that Oscar almost burst into tears, but he managed to crane his neck and breathe in heavily, stemming the flow.

'I will, I just need to do something first,' Oscar said in a hoarse voice.

'Can it wait?'

'I don't think so.'

The priest's grip lessened, but his hand remained.

'We play with our time in such a dastardly manner. With which, we might trade for eternity one of these days.'

Oscar looked to the gravestones, many of which rose like dark monoliths in the fog, but not all; some lay in a sorry state of disrepair. Their etched words now blotched, with weeds encircling their bases. None left on this earth to tend to the deceased, their bloodline ended, and any friends and acquaintances who once remained, gone too.

'God is not the author of confusion, but of peace,' the priest said.

'And I am confused,' said Oscar.

He cast his head down, signaling for the priest to remove his grip.

'I should leave,' Oscar said. Gesticulating a smile as his firm goodbye.

'I am sad to see you go,' the old man said.

Oscar trudged through the dense fog to the outskirts of town. Here, the road turned into a well-trodden track. He saw no vehicles enter or leave the town on his journey, for the foggy conditions were too hazardous. He followed the country road South for some way, perplexed by his surroundings despite their familiarity. The density of the fog had created an otherworldliness; one that blurred between familiarity and the queer. Hedge tops hung over the road at either side of him, and he struggled to believe, even on a clear day, that a car might ever make it down this track without ending up in a ditch.

Eventually, he arrived at a crossroads. The fog became increasingly dense here, and he could only make out he had arrived by way of the hedges separating at either side of him. He remained still and stretched his hands before him, losing sight of his fingers in the fog.

He heard a faint, pitch-perfect whistling approaching him, unlike any tune he had ever heard. Though, he could not determine from which direction the tune was emanating from.

'Oscar.'

The stranger appeared from the fog, as though he pulled his form from an invisible marsh, revealing each limb to Oscar separately, until he stood in his entirety mere inches away.

The stranger's features were reminiscent of an Enlightenment sculpture. His eyes a virulent green; a green that carried an intoxicating charm. His hair was a strident black which fell atop his shoulders, curling inwards, a brilliant silver sheen reflecting from which through the light of the mist. He looked both boyish and archaic and wore a black raincoat. The mists folded round the tails of his coat, allowing his silhouette to be perceived more fairly. Adding to the illusion he had just impossibly climbed through a mirror to the other side.

The man was most pleased at the sight of Oscar, lunging at the opportunity to shake his hand. Oscar realised this most peculiar; it was as though for some reason, this meeting was not to take place, and as such, the exchange was now an excitable affair.

The stranger grasped his hand like a proud father, applying a slight pressure to his grip that matched Oscar's own.

Oscar pulled his hand away and turned his expression to one of disrepute.

'Have you got it?' Oscar asked abruptly.

'I have,' the stranger said, not moving nor indicating any sign he would retrieve anything for him.

'Can I, have it?' Oscar asked assumingly.

'Yes.'

Oscar retrieved his wallet; the notes almost spilling to the ground as he opened it. The stranger took the money from him, keeping his eyes trained on his Oscar's beaten face like an owl. From his other pocket, he withdrew a silver gun and aimed it directly at Oscar's head.

Oscar's purple cheek flinched as he braced himself to be shot square in the face, all the while trying to not appear afraid.

'It has a safety lock on it, do not fear,' the stranger said, looking at the back of the gun. 'My mistake, it does now!'

The stranger roared with laughter, the tip of the man's nose pointed to the sky and his lips peeled back to reveal his canines. The rich sound of his cackle echoed across the surrounding plains.

The stranger pressed down on a switch towards the back of the firearm, but he moved his hands with such speed, the movement appeared only to Oscar as a blur in the mist.

Oscar sheepishly returned to his heels, hesitant to ask about the gun's safety lock.

The stranger dropped the gun into Oscar's palms, pulling his fingertips back sprightly before they touched his.

Oscar took the weapon timidly, tossing it gently between his hands, as though to suggest he knew what he was doing.

'Is it loaded?' he asked, gripping the handle, raising the gun up and down, as if he was surmising its weight.

'Yes. I would not supply you with a gun that you could not shoot. I am not a cruel benefactor,' the stranger said, sullenly.

Oscar's frown broadened. He looked to the man's viridian eyes, searching for any sign of falsity. Alas, he could not perceive anything more than the sea of green.

The stranger held his gaze, amenable to it.

'Your brilliance sings, whilst other's hums,' the stranger said.

Oscar kept his eyes fixated on the gun.

'Do I need anything else?'

'Do you?' the stranger asked.

Oscar marched back from the junction, the mist clearing by the time he made it to the outskirts of Kellwell. The eve now dawned and purple streaks shot about the sky. He was tired but had acquired a renewed sense of purpose with the gun fastened under his trousers. It was held in place, only, between his jeans and his leg. He cursed himself for his lack of preparation, but a part of him assumed he would never have gone so far as to obtain the weapon.

It came as a surprise to him; he had little fear of being caught with the gun. And had a burgeoning excitement within him, pertaining to his newfound ability to shoot someone. However, the anxiety of being caught quickly became a pressing matter when he arrived in the town centre. Many bodies were now milling about the streets, and he was uncertain if these people had always been present in the mists, awaiting him.

He made sure to push his hand against his jeans, as to steady the weapon whilst ascending the hill, becoming conscious of his predicament. Hobbling through the street, covered in wounds, clutching at something which was jutting out from under his trouser leg, resembling something remarkably similar to a gun. He wondered how many people had trotted a gun through Kellwell; he may be the first. And on this basis, he was confident that those who surrounded him would guess the gun to be a thousand other things, before they guessed correctly.

He arrived home without so much as a second look from anyone and went up to his room. He took off his trousers first, whilst crudely holding the weapon over his jeans. He was under the impression that the safety was on, but this did little to console him.

As his trouser leg came free from him, he delicately pulled the gun from its position and lay it on the bed. It was heavier than he first thought and made quite the impression on his blood studded mattress. The gun nozzle faced the pillows at the top of the bed, and he wondered what sound the bullet would make if it were to pass through the pillows. The cushions surely would do little to stop the bullet, but would they slow its trajectory in a meaningful way? He was altogether unsure, but speculated, nevertheless.

He wanted to try shooting the thing but could not assure himself it was wise. He did not know how loud the gun shot might sound. If he was to stand in his closet and fire the gun into the floor where his clothes lay bundled, would the bullet travel through these layers, then the wood, and then bedroom floor below it?

He took the firearm once more in his left hand, and with his right, gently thumbed the crumpled paper that remained on his bedside table. He wished to read the contents of the page but decided it best he did not. Now, was not the time for contemplation.

He lay still on his bed for a hazy amount of time, making the decision to not change his clothes, only leaving his room to visit the toilet. Which he did, a total of twice. Each time, he urinated with stifled grunts, seams of red blood accenting his dark urine. On another day, this would have concerned him.

He took back his place on his bed, resting the silver gun beside him. With one hand he occasionally visited it. He sighted less webs hanging from his ceiling this evening; perhaps the chilly breeze from his window had knocked them down, and they now remained invisible, surrounding him.

In the dead of night, he rose from his bed. He had not slept; lassitude no longer affected him. He searched his wardrobe, drawing from it, a black backpack, to which he placed the silver gun into. He slung one strap over his shoulder; he always felt diminutive and rather sorry for himself when two straps were worn. He wondered if others thought of this phenomenon similarly.

He descended the stairs, exiting his home, stepping out to the grim night. The gentle buzzing of streetlamps was the only sound present. The air was hiemal, and there was no wind. The stars dwindled, unable to outshine the light of the town.

Oscar descended the hill at a brisk pace, his head firmly hunched between his shoulders under his cap. He pulled his hood over himself, like a black cowl which enveloped him; the fabric sagged round his cheeks, and positioned itself just before the brim of his hat. His movement felt light, unhindered for the first time today. He walked past the cathedral, and looked to the grand spires which circled its foundation, they stretched high into the night, like warped towers; sublime and daunting. The street was empty and not a single spirit crossed the road before him or made their way to him.

He arrived at the bench at the bottom of Eva's estate. He sat on it, and looked directly across to the opposite street, before summoning the will to look to his right. There, he saw the battered silver car, parked, where it should be.

He rose from the bench, allowing his hand to run against the splintered wood beside him, feeling every crevice and crack etched within. Softened only in places where one would sit. In places one would not, splinters alike daggers protruded, so small and slight that one would not notice them unless they were to press their palm firmly against the wood.

He walked towards the silver car and took a right.

He stood outside Eva's home. Her window ever ajar, even during this frigid night. It would take a fimbulwinter storm to swallow up the inhabitants of Kellwell and arrive at her door, before she were to shut it. And even then, she would look to this great icy storm in peril, asking her father, first, if she were to shut her window. As if this act alone, might solicit the passing of the tempest.

Her family's car was not present on the drive.

He gripped the shoulder of his backpack. Should he remove the gun from the bag and climb onto the garage roof? This posed some difficulty, as having the gun on hand would make the maneuver more challenging. Or should he bring the bag up with him? This meant he would have to unzip the bag once inside the house, which would be loud and sure to disturb.

He decided the most appropriate solution was to leave the bag partially unzipped with the gun inside. Although this raised the potential of the gun falling from the bag if his maneuver was at all haphazard. Though, if he was careful, it would be a success.

He took one last look at the brightly lit street, and briskly jogged to the garage. Jumping forth, he found purchase on the above platform, pulling himself onto it with ease. He removed the gun from the bag, leaving it here.

A short trip now presented itself across to Eva's window. With one hand steadying him, the other on the gun which he gripped as tenderly as the night, he shimmied across the jutting roof overhanging the living room.

He now stood on the ledge, outside Eva's window. Her curtains were drawn, as expected. With one leg, he mantled over the outer sill, and sat on the window stool composing himself as if on horseback. He pulled the window open further and swung his remaining leg into the house. His eyes fixated on the gun as he brought his remaining arm inside.

His boots touched down on Eva's carpet. The interior of the room was pitch black. He stood upright, tilting his head downwards, as though this adjustment would provide added concealment. With both hands, he held the handle of the gun and aimed the barrel into the darkness, his tender grip fiercening. His arms would have to be severed from his torso for any to claim the weapon from him. His eyes darted across the abyss, in hope of a familiar sight. He doubted if he was in the right house, his pupils unable to adjust to the dark. He did not wish to approach the bed, as he had not heard a single stir from it. And now, he was unsure if anyone else was even present. He could not remember this place being so devoid of light.

Outside the house, a car drove by; the gleam of its headlights entered the room, spilling across the window. If the driver were to be looking up at the window at this moment, they would be privy to the sight of a hunched silhouette wielding a gun.

The light revealed the bed to Oscar that held the lovers. They did not stir, and he did not hear a breath from them. Their bodies looked deceased; they lay motionless. Eva lay closest to him, a mere foot away, her pale face still and her russet hair cowped over her. Behind her, lay Red, his hands wrapped around her burgeoning white breasts.

Once more, all went black as the car continued up the road. He shook violently, drawing the gun before him into the depths of darkness that affronted him. He aimed it somewhere at the bed, gripping it so tightly, he thought he might feint.

He remained stationed by the window, fixated, his grip never lessening. He was either waiting for another car to pass by, or something else. Of which, he was not entirely diffident.

His finger sat restlessly upon the trigger and his calves stiffened. The weight of the gun was unbearable. The bearing of it so strenuousness, his shoulders shook vehemently.

All was still.

PART THREE - LIMERENCE

CHAPTER NINE

DAWN

Oscar departed from the window, scaling back across to the garage roof to where his backpack lay. He picked it up and placed the gun back within. From here, he leapt to the ground and broke into a light jog.

He retraced his steps back through Kellwell, stopping only outside the cathedral. He thought of his friend, and wondered if he was still walking across the silent grounds. He cast his eye over the shadowy graves, looking aimlessly upon them, hoping to catch the attention of the priest a final time. Perhaps the priest was the man who rang the church bell? What an impressive feat, he thought.

He departed, hoping to feel a grasp upon his shoulder as he turned to walk the remaining distance home. With a resounding breath, he unlocked the front door to his home, freeing himself only, from the chill of the night.

He watched the sunrise from his bed. Shades of royal reds and a symphony of orange appeared, tinged by a sickly yellow. The sunburst hues gave way to the sun, which poked through a breaking of clouds. The glow was reminiscent of a kindling fire. It was peaceful, but he had seen enough. As with all things, they are only a variance on another thing. Nothing can exist in a vacuum, after all.

He pushed his back against the landing wall, taking up his position once more, aligning himself with the maroon impression still visible from the other night. The gun now rested peacefully on his lap, and he bent his legs before him, creating a makeshift cup out of his crotch for the weapon.

He thumbed the gun gently, tilting the barrel to face his leg. He ran his free hand across the landing floor, as if grazing the surface of the sea. He happened upon a petal stuck between the wooden panels, sundered from his mother's lilies. He held the petal, looking at its speckled white colour, before releasing it, allowing it to return to its rightful place. The petal floated down to the floor and made its way through the gap between the panels, disappearing into the dark of the below.

Oscar felt a heavy thud in one of his legs, followed by an abrupt noise. The sound couldn't have come from the gun; he was sure of it. Besides, he had no understanding of pulling trigger. He looked to the gun in confusion, attending to the weapon before his leg.

He scanned the gun intently, all the while, feeling a strange sensation of numbness overcome him. He peered over every nook and crevice the weapon had to offer. And at the side of its handle, he found a small black button that he assumed was the safety switch, which was depressed. He looked to his leg regretfully and saw an encroaching bloody pool spilling out from under it.

He closed his eyes. His bottom lip wobbled, and he cried.

His eyes were milky and weak, and he grew weary and cold. He missed those whom he had not spoken to and those who he did not wish to speak to.

He laughed in a muddle of tears, this ill fate proffering him with a final piece to his puzzle. He still had the strength to move and although he bled profusely, he did not feel as if he were to die.

He saw a framed picture of his mother, positioned to the side of her unmade bed on her desk. He had not seen it before and desperately wished to make his way over to it. He feared that the toil of movement may be his end, but he wished to see her face again.

He pulled himself up on the banister, heaving his form across the wooden floor, into his mother's room that existed across the landing. When inside, he allowed himself to fall forth onto her sheets, imprinting his bloodied hands on them, wrenching himself to the foot of her bedside table. The affair was now excruciatingly painful.

He looked at the picture of his dear mother. She was a beautiful woman when she was younger. Probably the same age as he was now. He thought how similar they looked, but how different. The expression she held carried a charming wavering, and contentment in her ambivalence. He pushed his cheek against the glass of the frame, giving his tears freely to his her. He squeezed the frame with his finger and thumb at either side of it, applying the minimum pressure needed to take it back with him to his resting place.

He knew he must return there.

He wheezed profusely. Yet, before letting himself collapse, he made his way to his bedside table. He knocked the mug to ground that rested atop the crumpled paper, and with great effort, picked the note up.

Now, to even move his leg slightly was to incur an unyielding throbbing.

He bled his way back to the landing and lay atop it. Beneath him, his blood made its way under his torso and cascaded down the gap between the floorboards. He heard the trickling strike the bottom of the depths repeatedly; the sound resembling the ticking of a broken clock.

His face shook and he was unable to stop it. He applied pressure to his gaping wound with his left hand, only now remembering the pressure might aid him.

He thought of what university he might attend, or if he even were to. What would he do with the rest of his days? He wished to write something.

He thought of his friends. He believed they would miss him, as they were not vicious. But this would be a disturbance at worst to them, there being little reason for his death to displace them entirely. They would go on about their trajectory unperturbed, seeking marriage and a family of their own.

He thought of Eva dearly, and he wished to rest his head once more on her winding body, her hair curling gently round his neck as they lay in a garth of white flowers under a gentle pink sky. Their backs supported by a great oak; the scent of the wilderness coupled with a midsummer's night.

Oscar's temperature rose and fell in quick succession, trickles of sweat dripping from his brow. He clutched the picture frame of his mother desperately. He thought to cry out for any to hear him, but the temptation soon passed when his pain dulled. He did not want to become a display of ignobility to the gathering ghosts. He closed his dreaming eyes and pushed the warm tip of the gun to his temple.

Oscar was not found by his mother. It had been reported to the police in the early hours of the morning that unsettling noises were heard from his residency. A runner who was passing by the house on the hill, had taken it upon herself to call the police. Within no time, an investigation was conducted, and a suicide was confirmed shortly after. The police recovered a gun and note from Oscar's remains. The note was provided to his mother, spelling the end of their investigation.

His funeral was a sombre affair, taking place in the Kellwell cathedral on the eve of Spring. Many of his family and friends were in attendance. The song of choice was a violin piece from a video game he used to play with his brother. Some wished for a lighter song to be chosen, but that was not fair to him. Oscar used to tell people in his lifetime that this would be the song of choice for his funeral, to the bemusement of his family and friends. It would be a shame not to grant him this.

Oscar's mother had informed select members of the crowd that a note had been left by her boy, but feared the lack of comfort its contents would provide. She told them he had declared his undying love for each of them. It was best this way.

Eva sat in attendance, alone, on the pew nearest the exit. Her dark makeup ran down her cheeks as the ceremony neared its end. She left early, as to not reveal herself to those in attendance.

Three rows ahead of her, Richard and Fred sat, who could be heard intermittently throughout the service.

Not long after Oscar's funeral, Fred would receive a diagnosis of Chrohn's disease. His condition would deteriorate over the years, and he would refuse to have a colostomy bag fitted. In this time, he had a significant relationship with a woman who lived locally. However, she soon declared she was no longer enamored with him; his addiction to hedonism and narcotics taking precedence. Fred died alone on the floor of a bedsit.

Richard would go on to have three children with Fran, purchasing a countryside home not far from Kellwell. It was not what Fran did for Richard, but what she did not do, that he loved. He would occasionally visit Oscar's headstone, making a seasonal trip to the cathedral, naming one of his three children after his deceased friend.

After a brief relationship with Red, Eva would depart from Kellwell and get a job working at a hospital in another part of the country. After a number of failed relations, she would go on to marry a man who worked there. Her and her husband would buy a house nearby and have two children.

When the ceremony ended, Oscar's mother exited the cathedral alone. She withdrew the crumpled note from her shoulder bag and read it for the first time.

Early in the morning, it was you who got dressed; I was waiting for the birds to let me rest.

I know it unfair that I hate you. For you are only guilty of making me toil for your love, whilst you receive mine freely. To stare into your eyes was to see the mirror of my hopes and dreams set fire before me. I know all who love cannot last, but when I was with you the heavens were set ablaze, if just for a moment.

There is naught I envy more than those who console in your arms, and to yearn for such is devastating. Now my legs can take me no further, and here I lie destitute in my own filth. I dream of all things which incite misfortune in my waking life, and only on these dreamed shores am I at peace.

For those who needed me had little use for me in their own lives, and in company, I escaped my isolation at the cost of my sanity. If I had one more day to live, I would do naught differently. That is not to say I drank from the pulp of life; it is to say I did not know how to live.

To my mother, in drudgery you lived to afford me life, and I wanted a world borne of my last breath for you. I thought my heart would heal, but it only healed into a thousand pieces. And, if this is all just a dream, I beg of you to let me sleep, for the winter will end but infinity bears me no relief.

In death, I know not where I go, so in warmth I take her cold hand.

With endless love,
Oscar

The bell chimed three and the crowd left the cathedral.

A priest walked the grounds, looking across the graves, searchingly.

Printed in Great Britain
by Amazon